His
SECOND
Chance

Mountain Rescue Romance, Book Four

MELISSA McCLONE

Cardinal Press, LLC
November 2018
ISBN-13: 9781944777166

Dedication

For Elizabeth Brooks

Special thanks to Dave Tucker, John Scurlock, Terri Reed, and Jennifer Shirk.

Chapter One

Dr. Cullen Gray trudged through the Wy'East Day Lodge, his sore feet entombed in climbing boots he couldn't wait to remove. His muscles ached after two grueling days on Mount Hood. But whatever he'd been through was worth the tiredness and pain.

A climber had been rescued.

That trumped a night spent in a warm, comfy bed, a hot shower in the morning, and a homemade breakfast complete with scrambled eggs, chicken-apple sausage, and buttermilk pancakes with huckleberry syrup.

The smell of coffee wafted in the air, the aroma tickling Cullen's cold nose and teasing his hungry, grumbling stomach. A jolt of caffeine would keep him going long enough to survive the rescue debriefing and the short drive home to Hood Hamlet.

Twenty feet in front of him, volunteer members of Oregon Mountain Search and Rescue, OMSAR, sat at a long cafeteria table with coffee cups in front of them.

Backpacks, helmets, and jackets were scattered on the floor.

Almost there.

Cullen couldn't wait to take off his backpack and sit, if only for the length of the debriefing.

He passed a group of teenagers, students at the Hood Hamlet Snowboarding Academy, who laughed while they took a break from riding. A little girl, around six years old and dressed in pink from her helmet to her ski boots, wobbled away from the hot chocolate machine holding a cup with both hands.

A few hours ago, a life had hung in the balance, cocooned inside a rescue litter attached by cables to a hovering helicopter. But down here, lower on the mountain, everything had continued as if what run to take on the slopes was the most important decision of the day. He preferred being up there, though not because of any element of danger or adrenaline rush. He took only calculated risks to help others and save lives.

Cullen lived simply in the quaint, Alpine-inspired village of Hood Hamlet. Work and the mountain comprised his life. Sometimes, the two were enough. Other times, they weren't even close. But days like today reminded him why he did what he did, both as a doctor and a volunteer mountain rescuer. Satisfaction flowed through his veins.

A successful mission.

It didn't get much better than that. Well, unless the climber hadn't fallen into the Bergschrund crevasse to begin with. But given the distance of the fall, the climber's serious injuries, and the technical nature of the rescue, Cullen thought Christmas magic—something Hood Hamlet was famous for—had been in play even though it was May, not December.

Either that or plain old dumb luck.

Cullen preferred thinking Christmas magic had been involved. Luck seemed too random. He might be a doctor, but living here for almost a year had opened his mind. Not everything could be explained and proven scientifically. Patients did sometimes defy their diagnoses and survive with no logical explanation.

As soon as he reached the table, he shrugged off his backpack. Gear rattled inside. Carabiners clinked on the outside. With the straps off his shoulders, relief shot straight to his toes.

The pack thudded against the floor. The sound echoed throughout the cafeteria, drawing a few glances from the skiers, riders, and tourists.

Let them look. Complain even. Nothing could ruin this day.

He removed his black parka with the white block letters spelling RESCUE on the sleeve, tucked it under one of the outside straps of his pack, and then sat. His feet felt as if they were sighing in delight at not having to support any weight.

"Nice work up there, Doc." Bill Paulson, another OMSAR member, sat on the opposite side of the table. He passed Cullen a cup of coffee from the extras sitting between them. "What you did in the Bergschrund to save that guy's life…"

Cullen bent over to loosen his boots. He didn't want anyone fussing over his actions, let alone another mountain rescuer. He didn't need the praise. The result— a life saved—was payback enough. "All in a day's work."

"Maybe in the emergency department but not inside a crevasse." Paulson raised his cup. "I'm buying the first round at the brewpub tonight."

A beer was in order after this mission. "You're on."

Zoe Hughes, the beautiful wife of OMSAR team leader Sean Hughes and an associate member of the unit herself, stood behind Cullen. "Want anything?"

Heat from the coffee cup warmed his cold fingers. "This is all I need."

"Let me know when you want a refill." Her blue eyes sparkled. "Rumor has it you were a real hero up there today."

He shifted in his seat. Some considered mountain rescue a reckless pursuit, but nothing could be further from the truth. Rescuer safety was the priority, no matter what the mission. "Just doing my job."

She touched his shoulder. "Sean doesn't think he's a hero, either. But you're all heroes. What you guys do, who you are, is the very definition of the word."

"That's why we always get the girls." Paulson winked. "You're going to be my wingman tonight, Gray. We're going to get so many numbers we'll max out the memories on our cell phones."

Paulson, a firefighter with Hood Hamlet Fire and Rescue, had a reputation of being a player. No one would accuse Cullen of that. He never expected to be living like a monk, but he had a good reason. One that would end soon enough. Until then…

He stared into his coffee, black and strong, fighting memories and resentment.

Going out and doing anything other than drinking a beer and eating a burger didn't appeal to Cullen. The one woman he wanted didn't want him.

Time to move on.

He understood that. Had even come to terms with it. But he saw no reason to frustrate or tempt himself with something he couldn't have right now.

He lifted his cup. "You'll get those phone numbers whether I'm there or not."

"True that," Paulson agreed. "But think of the fun we'll have together. Just so you know, I'm partial to blondes. Though I don't mind brunettes or redheads."

Zoe shook her head, her long hair swaying. "One of these days, Bill, you're going to have to grow up and realize women weren't put on this planet solely for your enjoyment."

Paulson flashed her a charming grin. "Not going to happen."

Zoe grimaced. "Too bad, because love does conquer all."

"Love stinks," Paulson countered.

Cullen would echo the sentiment if he didn't need

more caffeine. He sipped his coffee.

"Sometimes." A sigh seemed poised to float away from her lips at any moment. "But other times, it's pure magic."

Yeah, right.

Cullen drank more. Love caused nothing but heartache and pain. He'd stick with Christmas magic.

Zoe went to refill someone else's cup.

The din of conversation increased, and so did the number of people in the cafeteria. More rescue team members arrived. A photographer snapped pictures. Someone placed a plate of cookies on the table. Briefing time must be close.

He checked his watch. "What's taking so long?"

Paulson grabbed a chocolate chip cookie from the plate. "Hughes must be outside talking to reporters."

Cullen wasn't a big fan of the media due to the way they covered and dramatized rescue missions on Mount Hood. Whenever anything went down on the mountain, reporters and news trucks raced to the rescue operation's base at Timberline Lodge, eager to capitalize on some poor soul's misfortune to increase ratings, web page hits, or circulation.

His stomach growled. He reached for an oatmeal raisin cookie. "Better Hughes than me. I want no part of that feeding frenzy."

Paulson snickered. "Once the press finds out who was lowered into the Bergschrund…"

"How about we say it was you?" Cullen bit into his

cookie.

"I'm game," Paulson said. "Especially if the hot blond reporter from Channel Nine wants to talk to me again."

Cullen took another bite. Tasted like one of Carly Porter's cookies. Her husband had been on the mission, too. Jake owned the local Hood Hamlet Brewing Company. A pint of Porter's Wy'East Lager, with Paulson buying, would hit the spot tonight.

Sheriff's Deputy Will Townsend approached the table with Sean Hughes at his side. Concern clouded their gazes. Worry was etched in their features.

Cullen wrapped his hands around his coffee cup. He hoped the climber's condition hadn't worsened on the helicopter ride or at the hospital. The guy was married with two young kids.

"Hey, Doc." Will tipped his deputy's hat. "Cell phone off?"

"Battery died." Cullen wondered what his phone had to do with anything. He placed his cup on the table. "Not a lot of places to recharge up there."

Will's eyebrows drew together. "We've been trying to reach you."

Cullen's throat tightened. He recognized the serious tone and steady cadence. He'd used both when delivering bad news at the hospital. "What's going on?"

"You're listed as Sarah Purcell's emergency contact."

Hearing the name startled Cullen. His coffee spilled, spreading across the table. "Sorry."

Paulson grabbed napkins. "No worries, Doc. I've got it."

Cullen stood and faced the deputy. "What about Sarah?"

Will's prominent Adam's apple bobbed up and down. "There was an accident on Mount Baker."

"Accident?" Cullen asked.

A muscle twitched in Will's jaw. "The details are sketchy, but it appears Sarah was at the crater rim when a steam blast occurred. She was hit by rock and fell a significant distance."

Shock reverberated through Cullen's body. His vision blurred. The world tilted sideways.

A hand tightened around his arm. "Steady, Doc."

Hughes.

"Deep breaths," another voice said.

Paulson.

Cullen felt himself being seated.

Sarah. Please, God, not her.

His emotions swirled like a whirlpool. Fear and dread spiraled, one on top of the other. Nightmares from another time joined in. Images of his twin brother, Blaine, flashed with strobe-light intensity until Cullen thought his head would explode. He forced himself to breathe. "Is she...?"

What was happening? He was a doctor. Death was something he saw almost daily during his shifts at the hospital. But he couldn't bring himself to finish his sentence.

Will leaned forward. "Sarah's at a hospital in Seattle."
Not dead.

A hundred pounds of anxiety melted away from Cullen's bone-weary shoulders. Tears of relief pricked his eyes. He hadn't seen Sarah in over a year. Cullen wanted her out of his life, but he hadn't wanted anything bad to happen to her.

Will named one of the top trauma centers in the Pacific Northwest.

Cullen blinked, gaining control in an instant. He'd done his residency there. Sarah would receive top-notch treatment, but he needed to make sure it was the right care. A good thing Seattle was only a four-hour drive away.

He stood, nearly toppling over before he could catch his balance. Tired. He was tired from the mission. "I've got to go."

Hughes steadied him. "Not so fast."

"We've been getting updates," Will explained. "Sarah is in surgery again."

Again.

Not good.

Cullen's hands fisted. Surgery could mean anything from pinning a fracture to relieving pressure on the brain. Volcanoes weren't safe places. Being a volcanologist had put Sarah in danger before, but no serious injuries had resulted. Bumps, bruises, a few stitches. But this...

Cullen dragged his hand through his hair. He was a doctor. He could handle this. "Any prognosis yet?"

Hughes touched Cullen's shoulder with the strength of a rescue leader and the compassion of a friend. "She's in critical condition."

A snowball-sized lump burned in his throat. While he'd been on the mountain saving a life, Sarah had been fighting for hers.

Bitter-tasting regret coated his mouth. Oh-so-familiar guilt, too. He hadn't been able to help Blaine. Cullen had to help Sarah.

He couldn't waste any more time. Sarah needed someone with her, and he was all she had.

Cullen grabbed his pack. "I've got to get to Seattle."

Hughes touched his shoulder again. "Johnny Gearhart has a plane. Porter's arranging everything. I'm going to drive you home in your truck so you can change and pack a bag, then we'll get you there. ASAP. I promise."

A protest sat on the tip of Cullen's tongue. He hadn't lived in Hood Hamlet that long, unlike several of these guys who'd grown up on the mountain. He'd climbed, skied, drunk beer, and watched sports on television with them, but he relied on himself and didn't ask for help. He didn't need help. But Sarah did.

Swallowing the words he normally would have said, he tried a new one instead. "Thanks."

"That's what friends are for," Hughes said. "Let's go."

Cullen nodded once.

"I'm in." Paulson, carrying his gear, fell into step with

them. "So Sarah… Is she family? Your sister?"

"No," Cullen said. "Sarah's my wife."

Chapter Two

Where am I?

Sarah Purcell wanted to open her eyes, but her lids felt as if they'd been glued shut. No matter how hard she tried, she couldn't pry them open.

What was going on?

Something pounded. It took her a minute—maybe longer—to realize the noise was coming from her head. Maybe she shouldn't try opening her eyes again.

Her head wasn't the only thing hurting. Even her toenails throbbed. But the pain was a dull ache as if it were far off in the distance. Much better than being up close and personal like a battering ram pummeling her.

She'd been hurting more. A whole lot more. This was…better.

White. She'd been surrounded by white.

Cold. She'd been so cold, but now she was warm. And dry. Hadn't she been wet? And the air… It smelled different.

Strange, but it felt as if something were sticking out of her nose.

Beep. Beep. Beep.

She didn't recognize the sound, the frequency of the tone, or the rhythm. But the consistent beat made her think of counting sheep. No reason to try opening her eyes again. Not when she could drift off to sleep.

"Sarah."

The man's voice sliced through the thick fog clouding her brain. His voice sounded familiar, but she couldn't quite place him. Not surprising, given she had no idea where she was, why it was so dark, or what the beeping might be.

So many questions.

She parted her lips to speak, to ask what was going on, but nothing came out. Only a strangled, unnatural sound escaped her sandpaper-dry throat.

Water. She needed water.

"It's okay, Sarah," he said in a reassuring tone. "You're going to be okay."

Glad he thought so. Whoever he might be.

She wasn't sure of anything. Something told her she should care more than she did, but her brain seemed to be taking a sabbatical.

What had happened?

Clouds had been moving in. A horrible noise had filled the air. Swooshing. Exploding. Cracking. The memory of the teeth-grinding sound, worse than two cars colliding on the freeway, sent a shudder through her.

A large hand covered hers. The warmth of the calloused, rough skin felt as familiar to Sarah as the voice had. Was it the same person? She had no idea, but the touch comforted and soothed. Maybe now she could sleep.

"Her pulse increased." Concern filled his voice. He seemed to be talking to someone else. "Her lips parted. She's waking up."

Not her. He couldn't mean her.

Sarah wanted to sleep, not wake up.

Someone touched her forehead. Not the same person still holding her hand. This one had smooth, cold skin. Clammy.

"I don't see a change," a voice she didn't recognize said. Another man. "You've been here a long time. Take a break. Eat a decent meal. Sleep in a real bed. We'll call if her condition changes."

The warm hand remained on hers. Squeezed. "I'm not leaving my wife."

Wife.

The word seeped through her foggy mind until an image formed and sharpened. His eyes, as blue as the sky over Glacier Peak on a clear day, had made her feel like the only woman in the world. His smile, rare to appear but generous when it did, had warmed her heart and made her want to believe happy endings might be possible, even if she'd known deep in her heart of hearts they didn't exist. His handsome face, with its high forehead, sculpted cheekbones, straight nose, and dimpled chin, had haunted her dreams for the past year.

Memories rushed forward, colliding and overlapping with each other until one came into focus.

Cullen.

He was here.

Warmth flowed through her like butter melting on a fresh-from-the-oven biscuit.

He'd come for her. Finally.

Urgency gripped Sarah. She wanted—no, *needed*—to see him to make sure she wasn't dreaming.

But the heavy curtain, aka her eyelids, didn't want to open. She struggled to move her fingers beneath his hand. It had to be Cullen's, right?

Nothing happened.

A different machine beeped at a lower frequency. Another machine buzzed.

Cullen.

Sarah tried to speak again but couldn't. Whatever was stuck in her nose seemed to be down her throat, too. No matter. She was so thankful he was with her. She needed to tell him that. She wanted him to know how much…

Wait a minute.

Common sense sliced through the cotton clogging her brain.

Cullen shouldn't be here. He'd agreed divorce was the best option. He no longer lived in the same town, the same state as she did.

So why was he here?

Sarah forced her lips apart to ask, but no sound emerged. Her frustration grew.

"See," Cullen said. "Something's going on."

"I stand corrected, Dr. Gray," the other person said. "This is a very good sign."

"Sarah."

The anxiety in Cullen's voice surprised her as much as the concern. She tried to reconcile what she was hearing. Tried and failed. She wanted to believe he cared about her—that even if they'd both given up on their marriage, their time together hadn't been so bad he'd wanted to forget about everything.

Maybe it would help if she tried to let him know that now.

Sarah used every bit of strength she could muster.

A slit of light appeared. So bright. Too bright. She squeezed her eyelids shut.

The light disappeared as darkness reclaimed her, but the pounding in her head increased. No longer far away, the pain was in her face, as if someone were playing Whac-A-Mole on her forehead.

She gritted her teeth, unsure if the awful growling sound she'd heard came from her. Everything felt surreal, as if she were a part of some avant-garde indie film. She wanted out. Now.

"It's okay, Sarah. I'm right here." Cullen's rich, warm voice covered her like one of his grandmother's hand-sewn quilts. "I'm not leaving you."

Not true. He *had* left her.

16

As soon as she'd mentioned divorce, he'd moved out of their apartment in Seattle, taking everything of his except the bed. After completing his residency, he'd moved to Hood Hamlet, Oregon. She'd finished her PhD at the University of Washington and then accepted a post-doctorate position with MBVI—Mount Baker Volcano Institute—in Bellingham, a town in northwest Washington.

Another memory crystalized.

Sarah had been developing a program to deploy additional seismometers on Mount Baker. She'd been trying to determine if magma was moving upward. She'd needed more data. Proof one way or the other. Getting the information meant climbing the volcano and digging out seismometers to retrieve data. Putting in expensive probes that provided telemetered data didn't make sense with their limited funding and the volatile conditions near the crater.

The crater.

Sarah had been at the crater rim to download data onto a laptop and rebury the seismometer. She'd done that. At least, she thought so. Everything was fuzzy.

Apprehension rose. Anxiety escalated.

The rotten-egg scent of sulfur had been thick and heavy in the air. Had she retrieved the data or not? Why couldn't she remember?

Machines beeped, the noise coming faster with each passing second.

She tried to recall what had happened to her, but her

mind was blank. Pain intensified, as if someone had cranked up the volume to full blast on a television set and then hidden the remote control.

"Sarah." His voice, sharp-edged like fractured obsidian, cut through the hurting. "Try to relax."

If only she could. Questions rammed into her brain. The jackhammering in her head increased tenfold.

"You're hurting," Cullen said.

She nodded.

The slight movement sent a jagged pain ripping through her.

Her throat burned. Her eyes stung. The air in her lungs disappeared when she exhaled. Inhaling, she could barely take in a breath. A giant boulder seemed to be pressing down on her chest.

"Dr. Marshall."

Cullen's harsh tone added to her discomfort, to her fear. Air, she needed air.

"On it, Dr. Gray."

Something buzzed. Footsteps sounded. Running. Wheels clattered against the floor. More voices. She couldn't hear what they were saying, nor did she care.

She gasped for a breath, sucking in a minuscule amount of air. The oxygen helped. Too bad the hurting more than doubled.

Make it stop. Please, Cullen. Make it…

The fear dissipated. The pain dulled. The boulder was lifted off her.

By Cullen?

At times, he'd taken such good care of her, whether she wanted him to or not. If only he could have loved her....

Floating. Sarah felt as if she were a helium-filled balloon let loose and allowed to float away into the sky. Up, up toward the fluffy white clouds. But she didn't want to go yet. Not until...

"Cull..."

"I'm right here, Sarah." His warm breath fanned her cheek. "I'm not going anywhere. I promise."

Promise.

The word echoed through her fuzzy brain.

Promise.

They'd promised to love, honor, and cherish each other. But Cullen had withdrawn from her, putting his heart into his all-consuming work and nothing into her. He'd seemed so stable and supportive, but he wasn't as open as she'd originally thought, and he'd held back emotionally. Still, they'd shared some wonderful times and adventures together. A year living in Seattle. Climbing, laughing, loving.

But none of that had mattered in the end. She'd brought up divorce, expecting to discuss their marriage. Instead, he'd said okay to a divorce, confirming her fear he regretted his hasty decision to marry her. Not only had he been willing to let her go without a fight, but he'd also been the first one to leave.

That was why she couldn't believe Cullen was promising to stay now. Maybe not today, but tomorrow or the next day or the day after he would be gone, leaving her with only memories and a gold wedding band.

The knowledge hurt, a deep, heart-wrenching agony, worse than any physical pain she'd endured.

I'm not going anywhere.

A part of her wished Cullen would remain at her side. A part of her wished marriage vows exchanged in front of an Elvis impersonator had meant something. A part of her wished love…lasted.

But Sarah knew better. She knew the truth.

Nothing ever lasted. No one ever stayed. Even when they promised they would.

And with that thought, she let herself float off into oblivion.

Chapter Three

Sitting in Sarah's hospital room, Cullen lost track of time. His friends returned to Hood Hamlet after driving his truck to Seattle so he'd have transportation. They supported him via text and phone calls. His family offered to come, but he told them not to. They didn't need more grief in their lives, and that was all they would find here in spite of Sarah's progress.

This small room, four walls with an attached bathroom, had become his world except for trips to the cafeteria and a few hours spent at a hotel each night. And his world revolved around the woman asleep in the hospital bed.

He rubbed his chin. Stubble prickled his fingertips.

Maybe that was why this felt so strange. He was married to Sarah, but she'd stopped being his wife over a year ago. In Hood Hamlet, she hadn't existed to anyone he knew. Not until her accident.

He rose from his chair, wishing he could be

anywhere but here. Not even the familiar artificial lighting and antiseptic smell brought him comfort. He'd spent more time at hospitals than anywhere else during the past six years—longer if he counted his four years at medical school. But nothing could quiet the unease tying his stomach in figure-eight knots.

His anxiety made no sense.

Sarah's condition wasn't as serious as her initial prognosis had indicated. Antibiotics had cured an unexpected infection and fever. The nasogastric tube had been removed from her nose. Her cuts had scabbed over. The incisions from her surgeries were healing. Even her closed head injury had been relatively minor, with no swelling or bleeding.

Surely that had to mean…something.

Time to settle matters between them?

Cullen wanted to close this part of his life.

The woman lying in the hospital bed looked nothing like the beautiful, vibrant climber he'd met at the Red Rock Rendezvous—an annual rock-climbing festival near Las Vegas—and married two days later. He wanted this injured Sarah to replace the image he carried in his heart—make that his head. Her chestnut-colored hair, clear green eyes, dazzling smile, and infectious laughter had been imprinted on his brain along with memories of hot kisses and passionate nights. She was like one of those adrenaline-rushing, stomach-in-your-throat, let-me-off-now carnival rides. The kind that appeared exciting and fun from a distance, but once on, made him wonder what he'd been thinking when he handed over his ticket.

That had been his problem with Sarah.

He hadn't been thinking.

She'd overwhelmed him.

Too bad he couldn't blame eloping on being drunk. Oh, he'd been intoxicated at the time—by her, not alcohol.

Cullen crossed the room to the side of her bed.

He'd been trying to forget Sarah. He wanted to forget her.

He'd never pictured himself divorced, and having their marriage fail hurt deeply. Yet, thoughts of her entered his mind at the strangest of times—on the mountain, at the hospital, in bed. But he knew what would stop that from happening—divorce.

After the divorce, things will be better.

These past months, especially when he was angry, frustrated, or lonely, the phrase had become his mantra.

Sarah's good hand slipped off the edge of the bed. That must be uncomfortable. He placed her arm on the mattress. Her skin felt cold.

Not good.

Cullen didn't want her to catch a chill. He tucked the blanket under her chin.

Sarah didn't stir. So peaceful and quiet. Adjectives he would have never used to describe her in the past. She'd been fiery and passionate, driven, and always up for a challenge or adventure. Nothing, not even the flu, had slowed her down much.

The silence in the room prodded him into action.

Staring at Sarah wasn't what the doctor ordered. Her doctor, that was.

Dr. Marshall hadn't wanted her to sleep the day away—not that Sarah could with nurses coming and going. But she hadn't been too coherent when she woke up, and then she'd drifted to sleep like a newborn kitten.

Might as well get on with it. If she followed the same pattern, she wouldn't be awake for long. "Rise and shine, Lavagirl."

Saying her nickname jolted him. He used to tease her about being a volcanologist until he realized she loved the piles of molten rocks more than she loved him.

He would try again. "Wake up."

Sarah didn't move. Not surprising, given her medications. Maybe if he kept talking, she would wake up.

"So I…" Cullen had tried hard not to miss her. He shouldn't miss her. He'd missed the sex, though. But he was only human—emphasis on the *man* part of the word. "I've been thinking about you."

He'd told many families that talking to unconscious patients was important. Now the advice sounded stupid. But when it came to Sarah, he'd never been very smart.

Keep talking, Doc.

He struggled for something to say. His resentment toward her ran deep. Maybe if he started at the beginning of their relationship when things had been better, this wouldn't feel so awkward. "Remember that first night in Las Vegas, you wanted our picture taken in front of the slot machines? We got the photo, but we were also thrown out of the casino."

They had stood on the sidewalk, both laughing, unsure of the time because of the neon lights. Her laughter had rejuvenated his soul. She was so full of light and love he couldn't get enough of her.

"You glanced up at me. Mischief gleamed in your pretty green eyes."

He'd been enchanted, transported to the time when freedom and fun reigned supreme, when he and Blaine had been impulsive and reckless, goading each other into daredevil challenges and stunts, believing they were invincible.

"Then you kissed me."

Changing all the plans he'd had for his life in an instant.

Cullen hadn't been able to think straight from that moment on. He hadn't cared. Being with her was a total rush. Perfect. Nothing else mattered.

"The next night, we strolled past the Happily Ever After Wedding Chapel on the strip. You joked about going inside to make things official."

She'd said if they eloped now, he couldn't forget about her when they returned to Seattle or leave her standing at the altar after she wasted years of dating him and planning their big wedding. He'd promised he would never leave her like that.

The affection in her gaze had wiped out whatever brain cells remained in his head. For the first time since Blaine's descent into drugs, Cullen had felt whole, as if the missing piece of him that had died with his twin brother had been found in Sarah.

"I couldn't let you get away."

Cullen had pulled her through the chapel's double glass doors. Forgetting about his vow to take only calculated risks, he'd dived headfirst without doing his due diligence and performing a cost-benefit analysis. He hadn't weighed the odds or considered the consequences of marrying a woman he knew nothing about.

Common sense couldn't override his heart. She'd made him feel complete in a way he'd never thought he'd feel again. He'd been downright giddy when she'd accepted his impromptu proposal. The chapel had a wedding package that included a ride to and from the marriage license bureau. Less than an hour later, they strolled out with matching smiles and plain gold bands, the proud new owners of a marriage certificate.

A whim? A mistake?

More like a regret.

A big one.

In December, when everyone was kissing under the mistletoe in Hood Hamlet and he was alone, he'd wished he had never been introduced to Sarah Purcell.

But Cullen had.

He'd married her.

That was why he was here now. They were husband

and wife until a judge declared otherwise. He couldn't wait to be free, to get his life in order, and to put his plan back in place.

Cullen was scratching one thing off the list, though. He wasn't getting married again. Been there, done that—no need to repeat that particular disaster.

At least he would have Paulson to hang with. The guy was a confirmed bachelor, if there ever was one.

But until Cullen's divorce was final, he was stuck with a wife who'd wanted to talk, to fight, to slice open one of his veins and have him bleed out every single thought and feeling he'd ever had.

After the divorce, things will be better.

He wanted to hate her, but seeing her like this, he couldn't.

Despite everything that had gone wrong between them and his reservations over seeing her again, Cullen couldn't resist her pull. The devastation of hearing she'd been hurt would have taken him to his knees if Hughes hadn't held him upright. Even if returning to Hood Hamlet made logical sense, he couldn't leave Sarah alone.

Not when she was injured.

And not when she had no one else but him to be with her.

Cullen sat on the edge of Sarah's bed. "Your lips are dry."

He picked up a tube from the bed tray, removed the cap, and ran the balm over her chapped lips. She didn't stir. "Better now?"

As he set the tube on the table, a movement in his peripheral vision caught his attention. The blanket had slipped. She'd moved her unbroken arm again. "Sarah."

She blinked. Once. Twice.

Her eyes opened. She focused on him. Her mouth formed a perfect O. "You're still here."

Sarah sounded surprised but relieved.

Her reaction offended him. "I told you I wasn't going anywhere."

Grabbing his hand, she squeezed. "You did."

Heat emanated from the point of contact, shooting to the tips of his fingernails and sparking up his arm. He expected her to let go. Instead, she stared at him. The corners of her lips curved upward hesitantly.

O-kay. It was a simple touch. Out of gratitude for his being here. No big deal. Except the heat tingled. It felt good. Too good.

Cullen pulled his arm away. "Thirsty?"

She nodded. "Water, please."

After he pushed the button that raised the head of her bed, he reached for the cup sitting on the bed tray and then brought the glass to her mouth. He positioned the straw against her lower lip. Even after the balm, her lips were dry and peeling. He remembered how they used to be so soft and moist and taste so sweet.

Don't think about that.

There weren't going to be any more kisses, no matter how much he'd enjoyed them in the past.

"Sip slowly," he cautioned.

Sarah did. She released the straw. "Where am I? What happened?"

The roughness in her voice scratched his heart. He held on to the glass of water. That would keep the temptation to brush the hair off her face at bay. "You're at a hospital in Seattle. There was a steam blast on Baker. You got hit by falling rock and fell."

Her mouth quirked. "Did the steam blast continue?"

"No." Not surprising she cared more about the volcano than herself. "But Tucker Samson—he introduced himself as your boss and the head of MBVI—said this could be a sign of an impending event."

Her eyebrows slanted. Beneath the bandage on her forehead, lines formed as if she were deep in thought. "I...don't remember much."

Sarah had a mind like a steel trap. She never forgot anything. He didn't blame her for sounding worried. "It's okay. You have a concussion, but it's a closed head injury. No brain trauma."

Panic flickered across her face. "I wasn't up there by myself."

"Two others were injured, but they've been released from the hospital. You took the brunt of it. Fell quite a distance."

Saying that was easy now, but the image of Sarah when he'd first arrived at the hospital haunted him. His uselessness then reminded him of trying to help Blaine— who had only wanted to blame Cullen for his drug addiction—and of trying to revive his brother after he'd overdosed. Being forced to watch from the sidelines as others treated Sarah was like having his heart ripped from his chest. He'd felt the same when the paramedics had arrived at their parents' house and pushed him away from his unconscious brother. But Sarah didn't need to know any of that.

A corner of her mouth rose into a more certain smile. "Guess that's why I feel like I've gone nine rounds in a boxing match."

"Mixed martial arts seems more your style."

"Yeah, now that you mention it, this does feel more like MMA than a few punches, hooks, and jabs."

She hadn't lost her sense of humor. That and her intelligence had been two of Sarah's most appealing traits. She'd had a hot body, too. The hospital gown and blanket covered much of her, but she'd lost weight. Her cheekbones appeared more prominent and she looked smaller, almost fragile, a word he never would have associated with her before.

He pushed the straw toward her lips again. "Drink more."

Sarah took another sip. "I've had enough. Thanks."

"Ice chips will soothe your throat. It has to be sore from the tube." He placed the cup on the bed tray. "Hungry?"

"No." A question formed on her face. "Should I be?"

She sounded nothing like the strong, independent woman he'd married. Her vulnerability tugged at his heart, twisting him inside out. He wanted to hold her until her uncertainty disappeared and she felt better. But touching her, even out of compassion, wasn't a smart idea. "Your appetite will return soon enough."

"Maybe my appetite doesn't want hospital food."

That was more like his Sarah. Wait, *not* his. "Then your appetite is one smart cookie."

She smiled.

Okay. This conversation was going better than he'd imagined. Maybe the bump on her head had shaken some sense into her. Not that Sarah's injuries changed anything between them. "I'll sneak in some decent food."

"I should eat even if I don't feel like it. I need to get to the institute to study the data."

What she said made him bristle. Sarah was a scientist, first and foremost. Studying volcanoes wasn't a job for her but a passion. The need to be where the action was happening was as natural an instinct as breathing to Sarah. Her work was for the greater good of science and mankind. If only she cared enough to put as much effort into her personal relationships.

Into him.

"Other scientists can analyze the data." He wouldn't let Sarah sabotage the healing process. "You need to recover first."

"I'm the institute's specialist. They need me. Those are my seismometers up there."

"Yours?"

Her lips pursed, but not in the kiss-me-now way she

31

had perfected. "A grant paid for them, but the data... Was the equipment damaged?"

"Tucker said the equipment was recovered. The data from the laptop is being analyzed."

"Thank goodness." She glanced around the room until her gaze landed on the door. "How soon until I can get out of here?"

He held up his hands, palms facing her. "Not so fast."

"We may be able to use the data to figure out what's going to happen on Baker. If we predict an eruption successfully, we can use the same process with other volcanoes and save lives."

Her passion flowed out like hot lava. Cullen understood why she was so adamant about her work. He felt the same about his. But he had to play devil's advocate, even if he wanted nothing more than to send her on her merry way to Bellingham. "The concussion is only one of your injuries."

Sarah glanced at her body, as if finally realizing she was more than a talking head. She focused on the cast on her right arm. "I can slog up Baker with a sling."

As ridiculous as the image of her doing that was, he could see her attempting it. She would hurt herself again. Given the pain medication she was on, she could misjudge distances. She might not survive another fall. "How will you self-arrest if you slip? It's difficult enough to dig in an ice ax to stop yourself with two usable hands and arms."

Moistening her lips, she lifted her chin with defiance. "I won't need to stop myself if I don't slip."

A smile threatened to appear at her bravado. He pressed his lips together. The last thing he wanted to do was encourage her. "You suffered internal injuries, a collapsed lung, broken ribs, and an arm fracture. Not to mention you've had two surgeries."

"Surgeries?"

"You have a pin in your right arm, and you no longer have a spleen. Due to the trauma and bleeding, they had to remove it with an open procedure rather than using laparoscopic techniques."

"Oh." Sarah was reacting as if he'd told her she'd overslept her alarm, not had an internal organ removed through a four-inch incision. "You don't really need a spleen, right?"

A groan of frustration welled inside him. Why couldn't she be one of those ivory-tower-type scientists who worked in a lab and never cared if they breathed fresh air or saw sunlight? Then again, he wouldn't have been attracted to someone like that. "You can survive without one."

"That's a relief." She touched her cast. "How soon before I can get back to the institute? Next week?"

Try four to six weeks, if everything went well with her recovery. Most likely six to eight with the surgery. But he reminded himself he wasn't in charge of her medical care. "You'll have to ask your doctor."

Her gaze pinned him. "You're a doctor."

"I'm not *your* doctor."

"You have to have some idea."

Cullen had more than an idea. But he wasn't here as a medical professional. He was here to support her, even if he wasn't part of her life anymore.

He'd been surprised to find out he was her only emergency contact. She'd mentioned her parents to him once, saying they were no longer a part of her life. He supposed the blank line on the employment form had needed a name, any name. No one ever thought the person listed would be contacted. "More than a couple of weeks."

She rubbed her lips together. "Guess I'd better talk to my doctor and find out."

"Once you know—"

"You'll go home," she finished for him.

Nothing had changed. She wanted him out of her life. He would be happy to accommodate her. "Yes, but not until you're out of the hospital."

Leaving her alone until then wouldn't be right.

"Thank you." Her voice dropped to a mere whisper. "Thanks for being here. This had to have messed up your schedule."

Sarah's unexpected sincerity curled around his heart and squeezed tightly, like a hug. He shifted his weight between his feet. "My schedule doesn't matter."

She faced him with an intensity he knew well. She might be bruised and battered, even broken, but intelligence and strength shone in her gaze. Her eyes were what he'd noticed first about her when they'd met over morning coffee at a campfire.

"Your schedule matters," she countered. "It always has before."

"I don't want you to be alone." That much was true. "You're still my wife."

Her face paled. "My fault. I've been so busy at the institute I never followed through on my end with the divorce. I'm sorry. I'll have to get on that."

After bringing up a divorce, she'd been too busy slogging up and down Mount Baker in the name of research to file the marriage-dissolution paperwork. He rubbed his neck. "No need."

Her lips parted. "What do you mean?"

A part of him wanted to get back at Sarah, to hurt her the way she'd hurt him.

You're a great guy. You'll make some woman a fantastic husband. But our eloping was impulsive. I acted rashly. Didn't think about what I was doing. Or what would be best for you. I'm not it. You deserve a wife who can give you the things you want. Things I can't give you.

Correction. Things she didn't *want* to give him.

Regret rose like bile in his throat. "I knew you were busy, so once I established residency in Oregon, I contacted an attorney to file there."

"Oh." Her focus on him never wavered. "Okay."

Nothing about this felt okay to him. The knots in his stomach tightened. His throat constricted. He'd had their entire future planned out. A house, pets, kids. And now...

Putting Mount Rainier, Mount St. Helens, Mount

Adams, and Mount Hood between Sarah and him had never appealed to Cullen more. "I'll go see if your doctor is around so we…you…can find out when you might be discharged."

He strode toward the door without waiting for her reply.

"Is it okay to use the bathroom?" Sarah asked.

Cullen stopped, cursing under his breath. He needed to help Sarah. But the last thing he wanted was to touch her, to hold her. What if he didn't want to let go?

Being angry didn't mean he wasn't still attracted to her. He would have to be careful.

With a calming breath, he glanced over his shoulder. "Yes, but not on your own. I'll grab a nurse."

Cullen exited the room. He could have hit the call button, but he needed some distance, if only for as long as it took to reach the nurses' station.

He would let the nurse determine the best way to get Sarah on her feet. If he was pressed into service, so be it. But he hoped the nurse was one of the practical types who would handle things herself.

The less he had to do with Sarah until her release, the better.

Chapter Four

Feeling as if half her brain and body weren't functioning, Sarah washed her hands in the bathroom sink.

A blond nurse named Natalie hovered nearby. Dressed in blue scrubs, the woman never stopped talking or smiling. "After surgery and pain meds, your system will need time to get back to normal. But you're doing great already!"

Heat rose in Sarah's cheeks. She wasn't used to being congratulated for using the toilet. Maybe when she was a kid, but knowing her parents, she doubted it. At least Natalie had given her *some* privacy. Having the nurse help was better than Cullen, even though he was stationed outside the door.

Don't think about him.

She dried her hands, wishing every movement didn't take so much effort or hurt so badly. "Um, thanks. I'm not used to my bathroom needs being a community event."

"Don't be embarrassed. This is nothing compared to labor and delivery." Natalie sounded like she had a few stories to tell. "There's no room for modesty there."

Sarah couldn't imagine. Nor did she want to. Given she had no desire to marry again, she doubted she would ever set foot into a labor and delivery room. Unlike Cullen. If ever a man was meant to be a father…

An ache deep in her belly grabbed hold of her, like a red-tailed hawk's talons around his prey, and wouldn't let go. She struggled to breathe.

Her incision. Maybe her ribs. She leaned against the sink to allow the pain to pass.

Natalie placed a hand on Sarah's shoulder. "Sit on the toilet."

A knock sounded. "Need help?"

Cullen's voice stopped whatever had been hurting. Sarah straightened. "I'm fine."

Natalie adjusted the ties on the gown. "Let's get you back before Dr. Gray gets on me for keeping you away too long. Doctor hubbies are the worst, since they're sure they know what's best for their wives."

Maybe some doctors, not Cullen. He'd looked as if he wanted to bolt earlier. She didn't blame him. This was the height of awkwardness for them both.

Natalie opened the bathroom door. "Here she is, Dr. Gray."

Sarah shuffled out. Each step brought an ache. A pain. Squeezing sensations. Nausea, too.

Cullen held out his arms slightly, but he wasn't spotting her as closely as before. Dark circles under his eyes and stubble on his face made her wonder how much sleep he'd been getting. Not much, based on his appearance. But he was still the most handsome man she'd ever seen.

The thought bothered her. She shouldn't be thinking that way about her future ex-husband. Maybe the pain medication was the reason.

"You're getting around better." He sounded pleased.

A burst of pride shot through her. "Just needed to find my legs."

"It's awful when they go missing," Natalie joked. "You two should take a short stroll down the hall. Sarah needs exercise."

Excitement spurted through her. She would love to get out of this room.

Cullen's lips narrowed. His expression suggested he didn't want to go anywhere with her.

Disappointment shot straight to the tips of her toes, even though he had every right to feel that way. Why would he want to spend more time with her than he absolutely had to? She'd hurt his pride by bringing up a divorce. As if shutting her out of every part of his life outside the bedroom hadn't hurt her. But she'd had to do something. It was only a matter of time before he dumped her. She'd saved them from suffering more hurt in the future.

"You should be walking a few times each day,"

Cullen said.

Of course he had to say that. He was a doctor. But he'd done enough. She wasn't about to force him to escort her.

Sarah padded toward the window. "I'll parade around the room. This gown isn't made for public appearances unless I want to flash the entire floor."

"I doubt anyone would complain." Cullen's lighthearted tone surprised her. "Especially not Elmer, the eighty-four-year-old patient two doors down."

Natalie laughed. "Elmer would appreciate it. He's such a flirty old man. But I'm sure you don't mind seeing her in the gown yourself, Dr. Gray."

Cullen winked at the nurse. "Well, Sarah *is* my wife."

Dumbfounded, Sarah stared at him. Legally, she *was* his wife. But he wanted the divorce as much as she did. Why was he joking around as though they were a couple?

He strode to the cupboard that resembled a built-in armoire with a drawer on the bottom. "And since I'd rather not have any men leering at her, it's a good thing I bought this."

Sarah had no idea what he was talking about. "What?"

Cullen opened one of the cupboard doors and then pulled out something orange and fuzzy. "This is for you."

She stared in disbelief at a robe. "I…"

"I hope orange is still your favorite color."

She was touched he remembered. "It is."

Natalie clapped her hands. "How sweet!"

His gesture sent a burst of warmth rushing through Sarah. This was so...unexpected. She cleared her throat. "Th-thanks."

"Now your backside will be covered, and I won't have to get into any territorial pissing matches." He held up the robe so she could stick her good arm through the sleeve. "Let's drape this over your right shoulder so we don't bother your cast."

Sarah nodded, not trusting her voice. She appreciated Cullen staying with her at the hospital, but she didn't want him buying her presents, especially ones as lovely and as thoughtful as this robe.

He tied the belt around her waist. "Now you're set."

She didn't feel set. She felt lightheaded. Chills ran up and down her arms. Neither had anything to do with her injuries, but everything to do with the man standing next to her.

"Ready?" he asked.

No, she wasn't.

"Go on," Natalie encouraged. "You can do this."

No, Sarah didn't think she could.

Cullen extended his arm toward her. She reached for his hand, unsure if touching him would hurt, but she was too wobbly not to accept the help.

He held her arm, sending tingles shooting toward her shoulder. "It'll be okay."

Chills and tingles were not okay.

"I won't let you fall," he said confidently.

Sarah had no doubt he would catch her if her body

gave out and gravity took over. But who would stop her heart from falling for him? Or catch her if it did?

The last thing Cullen expected to become was Sarah's walking buddy, but that was what happened over the next three days. His reluctance gave way to anticipation for the after-meal strolls through the hospital corridors. He'd wanted to be here to help her. This offered him the perfect opportunity to do so.

They didn't discuss the past. They barely mentioned the future unless it related to her recovery. Sometimes, they didn't say much at all.

Supporting her was enough.

For now.

As they ambled through the tall trees and flowering plants in the hospital's atrium, Cullen held Sarah's hand. A satisfied smile settled on his lips. "You did have the energy to make it down here."

"Told you so. This is better than the hallways upstairs." Sarah glanced at the skylights. The ends of her chestnut hair swung like a pendulum. Her bruises were fading, more yellow and brown than blue now. "I can't wait until I can go outside."

"It won't be long." Sarah appeared healthier. He squeezed her hand. "You're getting stronger every day."

Her eyes sparkled. "It's all this exercise."

He wished the reason was because of him.

Yeah, right. He wasn't foolish enough to think this time together meant anything. These walks were about her health, nothing else. "Exercise can be as important as medication in a patient's recovery. So can laughter."

She grinned. "So that's why you wanted to watch the comedy show last night."

"You laughed."

"I did, but my abdomen hurt. Still worth it. And I'm smiling now."

"You have a nice smile."

"Thanks." She looked at their linked hands. "Do you think I could try walking on my own?"

Cullen had gotten so used to being her living, breathing walker that holding her hand had become second nature. He shouldn't get used to it. He let go. "You've got this."

Sarah took a careful, measured step. And another.

He flexed his fingers, missing her warm skin against his. "Tomorrow you'll want to hop on a bike instead."

Her lips curved downward in a half frown, half pout. "I enjoy our walks."

"Me, too."

Her expression did a one-eighty. Her face lit up as bright as a summer day at Smith Rock. It took his breath away.

He rubbed his face. Stubble pricked his hand. In a rush to get to the hospital, he'd forgotten to shave again.

"But I have to be honest." She peered around as if

seeing who might be listening. "I'm ready to escape this joint."

"I don't blame you." Except once she was discharged, everything would go back to how it had been. They would live separate lives in different states. The realization unsettled him. "You should be released soon."

"Has Dr. Marshall mentioned when?"

The anticipation in her voice made Cullen feel foolish for enjoying this time together. She wanted a divorce. He wanted one, too. "No. But given your progress, Dr. Marshall might have one in mind. Ask him when he makes his rounds."

Hope filled her expression. "I will."

Sarah took another step, swaying. She stumbled forward.

"Whoa." Cullen wrapped his right arm around her, mindful of her sutures and ribs, and grabbed her left hand. "Careful."

She clutched onto him. "I lost my balance."

If that was the case, why was she leaning against him with her fingers digging into his hand? But he enjoyed the way she clung to him. "This is the farthest we've gone. Let's go back to your room."

He expected an argument.

Instead, she nodded.

Sarah loosened her grip, flexed her hand, and straightened her shoulders. "I can make it on my own."

Cullen laced his fingers with hers. "I know, but humor me anyway."

She held on. "I suppose that's the least I can do after all you've done for me."

A list of what he'd done scrolled through his mind. "I suppose it is."

Sarah owed him, and he would gladly take this as payback. He wasn't letting go of her. That had nothing to do with how good having her close felt. He caught a whiff of her floral-scented lotion. Or how good she smelled.

Nothing at all.

That afternoon, Sarah gripped the edge of the hospital blanket. Staring at Dr. Marshall, she wondered if she'd misunderstood him. She hoped so. "Don't you mean an independent discharge?"

"An independent discharge isn't going to happen." With his silver wire-frame glasses and thinning gray hair, Dr. Marshall resembled a grandfather more than one of Seattle's top surgeons, but the man was actually the devil in disguise. "You are unable to care for yourself. Your discharge planner and orthopedist agree."

She hadn't waited all afternoon only to hear this. "That's...silly."

Cullen, who leaned against the far wall near the window, gave a blink-and-you'd-miss-it shake of his head.

Her fingers tightened on the fabric, nearly poking

through the thin material. She hated being so aware of Cullen's every movement. Her senses had become heightened where he was concerned. She wondered if he felt the same way. Now she knew.

No.

Frustration tensed her muscles, making her abdomen ache more. Disappointment ping-ponged through her. They'd shared lovely times on their walks through the hospital while holding hands like high school sweethearts. She'd assumed Cullen would support her independent-discharge request, but he hadn't. He didn't want her staying by herself in Bellingham.

"Nothing about this is silly." Dr. Marshall kept an even tone though frustration was evident in his face. "You're lucky to be alive."

"No kidding," Cullen murmured.

She didn't feel that way. Plumes of steam rising from Mount Baker happened, but only bad luck could have put her at the crater rim during a steam blast. Now she was stuck in the hospital with only her soon-to-be ex-husband for company when she needed to be at the institute figuring out if the event was a precursor to an eruption or just the volcano displaying thermal unrest. "*Silly* was the wrong word to use, but I'm not an invalid. I'm getting around better."

Dr. Marshall gave her a once-over. "There's a big difference between walking the hallways and being capable of caring for yourself."

"You overdid it this morning," Cullen added, as if

dumping a carton of salt into her wounds helped matters.

"I have a ways to go in my recovery." She would be doing fine once the pain of her surgery incision and ribs lessened. The throbbing in her head, too. "But I don't need a nursemaid."

A knowing glance passed between the two men.

Sarah bit the inside of her cheek.

"No one is suggesting a nursemaid. But I agree with Dr. Marshall. You're right-handed." Cullen stared at her cast. "Dressing yourself, doing anything with your left hand, is going to take some adjustment. Not to mention your sutures and ribs. You'll need assistance doing everyday things. The limitations you'll have on lifting and driving will make getting to your follow-up appointments difficult."

Maybe she shouldn't have expected Cullen to take her side. But even with his lack of support now, she had no regrets. Bringing up divorce was better than waiting around for him to do it. And he would have. People always abandoned her. He would, too, once she was out of the hospital, leaving her alone.

Again.

The sinking feeling in her stomach transformed into a black hole, sucking her hope into the abyss.

No, she couldn't give in and admit defeat. The institute relied upon her expertise. Others had been analyzing the data since the steam blast, but volcanic seismology was her specialty. She couldn't let people down. Without her work, she had nothing.

Sarah glanced at Cullen. "I'll figure out a way. I need to get to work."

"Is your current and long-term health worth risking for a job?" Dr. Marshall asked.

She raised her chin. "If it means determining how to predict a volcanic eruption then yes."

A muscle ticked at Cullen's jaw. "If you go back to the institute too soon, you won't be doing them or yourself any favors."

Sarah saw his point, even if she didn't like it. "I'll be careful."

"What does your job entail, Sarah?" Dr. Marshall asked.

"Analyzing data."

"After she climbs Mount Baker to gather it," Cullen added. "Or am I wrong about that, Dr. Purcell?"

Of course he wasn't wrong. From his smug grin, he knew it, too. That was why he'd used her title. "I can send a team up to download the data."

Maybe that would appease him—rather, Dr. Marshall.

"Are you able to work remotely from home?" Dr. Marshall asked.

Sarah would rather be at the institute, but she would take what she could get. "Telecommuting is an option."

Dr. Marshall rubbed his chin. "Is there someone who can stay at your apartment and care for you?"

Sarah's heart slammed against her chest so loudly she was sure the entire floor of the hospital could hear the *boom-boom-boom.* Even though she knew the answer to his question, she mentally ran through her list of coworkers. Most would be happy to drop off food or pick up her mail, but asking one to stay with her would be too much. She couldn't impose on them.

She'd never had a close friend, a bestie, she could count on. Her life had been too transitory—shuttled between her parents and moving frequently—to develop that kind of bond with anyone. Not unless Cullen counted. She couldn't. It wouldn't be fair.

She chewed on her lower lip. "I'll hire someone."

"Home care is a possibility," Dr. Marshall said.

Fantastic. Except her studio apartment was tiny. The floor was the only extra place to sleep, the bathroom the only privacy other than a closet. She hated admitting the truth, but home care wouldn't work.

"If Sarah's in Bellingham, nothing will keep her from going to the institute or heading up the mountain if she feels it's necessary," Cullen said in a matter-of-fact tone.

She opened her mouth to contradict him but then clamped her lips together. What he said was correct.

His gaze challenged her. "You know I'm right."

Him knowing her so well annoyed Sarah.

"Is that true?" Dr. Marshall asked.

She tried to shrug, but pain shot through her. "Possibly."

Cullen laughed. The rich sound pierced her heart. One of Cupid's arrows had turned traitorous. "A one hundred percent possibility."

No sense denying it. He'd had her number since they met. Had it only been two years ago?

Dr. Marshall gave her a patronizing smile, as if she were a five-year-old patient who would appreciate princess stickers rather than a grown woman who wanted him to work out her discharge. "My first choice in cases involving a head injury, however minor, is home care by family members, but Dr. Gray mentioned your situation."

Sarah assumed Dr. Marshall meant their marriage, since Cullen was the closest thing to family she had. She wasn't an orphan. Her parents were alive, but they'd chosen their spouses over her years ago. "I'm on my own."

"That leaves a sniff. A skilled nursing facility," Dr. Marshall explained. "We call them SNFs. There are several in the Seattle area."

Cullen's smile crinkled the corners of his eyes, making her heart dance a jig. So not the reaction she wanted to have when she was fighting for her freedom. Independence. Work.

"That sounds like a perfect solution," Cullen said.

Maybe for him. In Bellingham, she had access to the institute and her own place to live. Down here in Seattle, she had...nothing. But what choice did she have? Sarah swallowed her disappointment. "I suppose. As long as I have my laptop and access to Wi-Fi."

Dr. Marshall adjusted his wire-framed glasses. "Most

SNFs have Wi-Fi."

"Your concussion, however, will make concentrating for any length of time difficult for you." Cullen sounded so doctorlike. Totally different from the man who had helped her to her room this morning. "If you push yourself, you may experience vision problems and headaches."

"I'll use a timer to limit my computer usage," she offered.

"No symptom is a one hundred percent certainty, but Dr. Gray is correct. You don't want to do too much too soon," Dr. Marshall said.

Something about his tone and eye movement raised the hair on her arms. "What exactly am I going to be allowed to do?"

"Rest and recuperate," Dr. Marshall said, as if those two things would appeal to her.

R & R was something a person did when they were old. Not when the second-most-active volcano in the Cascades might erupt. "The SNF sounds like my only option, but you might as well put me out of my misery now, because—"

"You'll die of boredom," Cullen finished for her.

In their one-plus year of marriage—over two if the time they'd been separated counted—he'd figured her out better than anyone else in her life. That unnerved Sarah.

Dr. Marshall adjusted his glasses. "A few weeks of

boredom is a small price to pay."

Small price? The SNF was probably an institutional cage. She'd be locked away. Forced to sleep or "rest." She stared at the cast on her arm.

Lucky to be alive. Maybe if she kept repeating the phrase, she would believe it. Because right now, her life sucked.

"There is another option," Cullen said.

Her gaze jerked to his. The room tilted as if she were standing in a mirrored fun house. She closed her eyes, realizing she must have gone too far earlier. When she opened them again, everything was back where it belonged. Cullen stared at her with an intense expression on his face.

She swallowed the lump of desperation lodged in her throat. Anything would be better than a nursing facility. "What other option?"

"Come home with me to Hood Hamlet."

Her mouth gaped. The air rushed from her lungs.

"I have Wi-Fi and a guest bedroom," Cullen continued, as if that made all the difference in the world. "I promise you won't be bored."

No, she wouldn't be bored. She would be struggling to survive and keep her heart safe.

Here at the hospital, people came in and out of her room. She and Cullen were never alone for long. Each night, he slept at his hotel. What would it be like if it were only the two of them?

Dangerous.

Sarah tried to speak, but her tongue felt ten sizes too big for her mouth, as if she'd been given a shot of Novocain at the dentist's office. But she knew one thing....

Going home with Cullen was a bad idea. So bad she would rather move into the SNF and die of boredom or stay in the hospital and die of starvation or go live in a cave somewhere with nothing but spiders and other creepy-crawly things for company.

Having him here made her feel warm and fuzzy. Taking walks reminded her of how comfortable they'd once been together. But she couldn't rely on him to be her caretaker. She'd been vulnerable before they'd separated. In his care, she would be at his mercy. If she found herself getting attached to him, or worse, falling in love with him all over again...

He would have the power not only to break her heart but also shatter it.

That would destroy her.

She couldn't allow that to happen.

Chapter Five

Cullen wore a digital watch but swore he heard the seconds ticking by. He braced himself for Sarah's rejection. He'd offered her a place to recover, but she'd reacted with wide-eyed panic as if she were about to be sentenced to life in prison.

Stupid.

He balled his hands with a mix of frustration and resentment.

Suggesting she go to Hood Hamlet had been wrong. But she'd looked so miserable over the idea of the SNF, he'd wanted to do something. A good attitude was important in a patient's recovery. He didn't want her to experience any setbacks. Skilled nursing facilities had their role in patient recovery, but Sarah was better off elsewhere. He knew that as a trained physician and in his gut.

But no one was going to step up to offer Sarah an alternative. No one except him.

And she hadn't even cared. At least not according to her anything-but-that reaction.

Might as well tattoo *sucker* on his forehead. He'd let their pleasant walks and hand-holding soften him.

A buzzing disturbed the silence.

Dr. Marshall checked his pager. "I have to go. Tell the nurse your decision and then have her relay it to me and the discharge planner."

The surgeon strode out of the room.

The minute the door shut, the tension in the air quadrupled. Cullen had faced challenges working as a doctor and as a mountain rescuer, but he'd never felt more out of his element than standing here with his wife—a wife who didn't want him for a husband. Not that he wanted her, either, he reminded himself.

Sarah toyed with the edge of her blanket. Her left hand worked fast and furiously as if she were making origami out of cloth.

The silence intensified. Her gaze bounced from her cast to the colorful bouquet of wildflowers from MBVI to everything else in the room. Everything except him.

Difficult to believe that at one time they were so crazy about one another they couldn't keep their hands or lips off each other. Now she couldn't bear to look at him.

He hated the way that gnawed at him. Time to face the music, even if a requiem played. "I'm only trying to help. Give you another choice."

"I'm surprised you'd want me around."

Her words cut through the tension with the precision of a scalpel. Cullen was about to remind her she had been the one to ask for the divorce. He held his tongue because she was right. He didn't want her around because she messed with his thoughts and his emotions, but he had to do the right thing here, whether he liked it or not. "I want you to recover. Get you feeling better and on your feet in the shortest amount of time possible. That's all."

She studied him as if she were trying to determine what type of volcanic rock he might be. "That's nice of you."

Her wariness bugged him. "We've been getting along."

Her lips parted. She pressed them together and then opened them again. "It's just…"

He hated the hurt squeezing his heart. "Would it be that awful for a few weeks?"

"No, not awful," she admitted. "Not at all."

Her words brought a rush of relief but added to his confusion. "Then what's the problem?"

"I don't want to be a burden."

A burden was the last label he'd use for her. "You're not."

"You've put your life on hold for me."

"I won't have to do that when I'm in Hood Hamlet. I'll have work and my mountain-rescue unit."

Sarah moistened her lips. "I thought I wasn't supposed to be alone."

"Friends have offered to help."

She avoided making eye contact. "So you won't be around that much?"

"I work twelve-hour shifts at the hospital. The rescue unit keeps ready teams stationed on the mountain in May and June."

"Oh."

That didn't tell him much. He rocked back on his heels. "So what do you think?"

"I appreciate the offer."

"But—?"

Sarah squinted. "I—I don't know."

Her uncertainty sounded genuine. He'd expected to hear a flat-out *no*.

She sank into her pillow. "Is it something I need to decide right now?"

"Dr. Marshall wants you to tell the nurse your decision. Arrangements have to be made if you choose a SNF."

She rubbed her thumb against her fingertips.

"Attitude plays a role in healing," Cullen continued. "Hood Hamlet will be better for you in that regard."

"Give me a minute to think about it."

Cullen didn't know why she needed more time or why he was trying so hard to convince her. Yes, he wanted to do the right thing, but her decision changed nothing. If she refused his offer, the next time they saw each other...

They wouldn't be seeing each other again unless she challenged the divorce terms. The way it would have been if she hadn't had her accident.

The bed dwarfed her body, making her appear small and helpless. Strange, given she was the strongest woman he knew next to Leanne Thomas, a paramedic and member of OMSAR.

Sarah grimaced.

Two long strides put him at the side of her bed. "Your head."

She gave an almost imperceptible nod. "I overdid it today."

His concern ratcheted. "Does anything else hurt?"

"Not any more than usual."

He touched her face. She wasn't flushed, but a temperature could mean another infection. "You don't feel warm."

"My brain might be rebelling from having to work again. Think I might need a nap."

"Probably."

But Cullen preferred to err on the side of caution. He checked the circulation of each finger sticking out from her cast. He wanted to blame his anxiousness on the Hippocratic oath, but there was more to his worry than that. The *more* part revolved around Sarah. Soon, he hoped—expected—not to care or to be so concerned about her. Time healed all wounds, right?

She opened her eyes. "You always had a nice bedside manner."

He didn't want what she said to mean anything. Hated it did. "It's easier with some patients."

"With me?" She sounded hopeful.

"Yes."

Sarah's lips curved into a slight, almost shy smile. "Thanks."

He brushed the hair off her face. "You're welcome."

Her eyelids fluttered like a pair of butterfly wings.

He remembered when she'd slept against him, her eyelashes brushing his cheek. The urge to scoop her up in his arms and hold her close as he once had was strong, but he couldn't give in to the temptation. This woman had trounced his heart. Whatever else he did, he couldn't let himself fall in love with her again.

"I'm not trying to be difficult," she said softly.

"You're being yourself. I wouldn't expect any less."

But he expected more from himself.

Seeing Sarah injured brought out his protective instincts, but he had to be careful. He had to be smart about this, about her.

She'd claimed to love him until the day she brought up divorce. She'd lied about her feelings. Let him down in the worst possible way.

He didn't trust her. He couldn't. No matter what she might do or say.

Memories and feelings he'd buried deep kept resurfacing. He preferred keeping his emotions under wraps, but losing control was too easy to do around Sarah. Once she declined his offer, he would be finished with her.

She blinked a few times. "I don't need more time to

decide. My goal is to recover as soon as possible. My apartment is too small for a caretaker to stay with me. A SNF would be too impersonal."

The implication of her words set him on edge. "So that means…?"

"I'll go to Hood Hamlet with you. If that's still okay?"

Not okay. His heart pounded and his pulse raced, as if he'd run to the summit of Mount Hood post-holing through four feet of fresh snow. An adrenaline rush from physical activity, no problem. Adventures with calculated risks, fine. The way he was reacting to Sarah? Unacceptable.

Still, Cullen had made the offer. He wouldn't take that back. But he would keep a tight rein on his emotions. He clenched his teeth. "It's fine."

Get Sarah home. Get her well. Get her back where she belongs.

Driving to Hood Hamlet on Highway 26, Cullen focused on the road and ignored the woman seated next to him. Not an easy thing to do with the scent of her sweet, floral lotion tickling his nose. That smell reminded him of all the things he'd missed about her.

He grasped the leather-covered steering wheel with his hands in the proper positions, exactly as he'd been taught in driver's ed. He'd rarely driven this way as a teenager. "Pedal to the metal" best described his and his brother's driving styles then. But after Blaine had overdosed, Cullen prided himself on doing things, including driving, the right way, the correct way, to make life easier on his grieving parents. He'd made stupid mistakes in the past, but he hoped he wouldn't make any more, especially where Sarah was concerned.

As he pressed harder on the accelerator to pass a semitruck, he fought the urge to sneak a peek at her. He'd done that too many times since leaving Seattle. Concentrating on the road was better. Safer. He flicked on the blinker to return to his lane.

"You haven't touched your milkshake," Sarah said.

The meaningless, polite conversation of the past four hours made him wish for a high-tech transporter beam that could carry them to the cabin in less than a nanosecond. He'd settle for silence, even the uncomfortable kind that made him squirm when he had nothing to say.

He stretched his neck to one side and then the other. "I'm not thirsty."

Cullen hadn't had much of an appetite since last night. Hadn't slept, either, tossing and turning until the sheets strangled him like a boa constrictor. He rolled his shoulders to loosen the bunched muscles.

She'd said she didn't want to be a burden, and she wasn't. Not really. But he was worried.

About her not healing properly.

About him getting attached to her.

About how saying goodbye would feel when she deserted him again.

"You're missing out." Sarah sounded as though she was smiling. "My chocolate milkshake is delicious."

A quick glance her way—he couldn't help himself—showed she wasn't. Her lips were tight.

She stirred her drink with the straw. "Thanks for suggesting we stop."

Stopping along the way had allowed her to change positions, but the detours had added time to the drive. "You need to stretch your legs."

Their final stop hadn't been about Sarah. The truck's cab had felt cramped. Confined. He'd needed fresh air and space.

"If you'd rather have chocolate, we can trade." She held out her cup. "Vanilla is one of my favorites."

Memories of other road trips to rock climb flashed through his mind. Stopping to buy two different kinds of milkshakes had become their routine. Sharing them during the drive had been the norm. Pulling over to make out or do more had been his favorite break. Hers, too.

Whoa. Don't go there. He tightened his grip on the steering wheel. "Thanks, but I'm good."

"Suit yourself, but I'm willing to share."

Her lips closed over the end of the straw sticking out of the cup. She sipped. Swallowed.

Sweat coated his palms. He needed to cool off. Quickly. "I'm happy with mine."

Cullen snagged his milkshake from the cup holder

and sucked a mouthful through the straw. The cold drink hit the spot. A few more sips and his temperature might return to normal.

He was much too aware of her—from the way she glanced sideways at him to the crooked part in her hair. Things he shouldn't notice or care about.

And he didn't. Care, that was.

But now that she was an arm's distance away, her feminine warmth and softness called to him like a PLB— a personal locator beacon—beckoning in the night. Only, no one was lost. Nothing was lost except the impulsive, reckless side of himself he'd buried with his brother. The side Sarah brought out in Cullen.

Sure, he missed the physical part of their marriage. What man wouldn't? But he'd been surviving without it. Without her. Celibacy was the better choice for now. Blaine had lost himself in drugs. Cullen had seen what losing control and addiction did to a man—to his brother. He wouldn't lose himself in Sarah.

He set his drink in the cup holder. Maybe if he didn't say anything to her, she wouldn't talk to him.

"Is Hood Hamlet much farther?" Sarah asked.

So much for that tactic. He gritted his teeth. "Twenty-five minutes if we don't hit any traffic."

"That sounds exact."

He'd been checking the clock on the dashboard every five minutes for the past two hours. "I drive this way to the hospital."

"You work in Portland, right?"

Great, more small talk. "Gresham. Northeast of the city."

"A long commute."

"Twelve-hour shifts help."

"Still a lot of driving," she said. "Why do you live so far away?"

He tapped his foot. "I enjoy living in Hood Hamlet."

"Aren't there closer places?"

"Yes, but I prefer the mountain."

"Why?"

Cullen focused on the road. "It's…"

"What?"

"Charming."

"You've never been one for charming." Doubt filled her voice. "You thought Leavenworth was, and I quote, 'a Bavarian-inspired tourist trap on steroids.'"

He had said that about the small town located on the eastern side of the Cascade Mountains. "I had fun climbing there."

"Nothing else."

He'd enjoyed spending time with her in Leavenworth. A glance at the speedometer made him ease up on the gas pedal. "Hood Hamlet is different."

"Different, how?"

Cullen thought about what he'd experienced over the past months. "There's something special about the town."

"Special?" Confusion laced her reply.

He nodded. "Almost…magical."

She half laughed as if the joke were on him. "When did you start believing in magic?"

He understood her incredulous tone. A year ago, he would have laughed, too. After Blaine died, Cullen hadn't believed in anything that wasn't quantifiable—whether it was a diagnosis or a cure. Everything had to have an explanation. The only thing in his life that defied reason—his relationship with Sarah—had blown up in his face. "It's impossible not to believe when you're there. A lot of people feel the same way."

"Must be something in the water," she joked.

A trained scientist wouldn't understand. Sarah's brain wasn't wired that way. He'd been the same way until three things had changed his mind—the rescue of two climbers trapped in a snow cave last November, the town pulling off its Christmas Magic in Hood Hamlet celebration in mid-December, and Leanne Thomas getting engaged on Christmas Day.

Those three events defied logic but had happened anyway. "Maybe."

"The mountain air, perhaps," she teased.

"You never know." But he knew neither of those things was the reason.

"Whatever it is, I hope it's not contagious."

"I have no doubt you're immune as long as Mount Hood remains dormant."

He expected her to contradict him, if only to argue with him. She didn't.

"What else does the town have besides magic?"

Sarah asked.

"The people. It's a great community." He hadn't realized how supportive they were until the numerous offers of help following her accident. "Very welcoming to strangers. That's how I ended up moving there. I'd driven up to Mount Hood on a day off. When I had lunch at the local brewpub, I met the owner, Jake Porter. When he found out I was involved with mountain rescue in Seattle, he told me about their local unit, OMSAR. He invited me to go climbing, and we did. He, his wife, and his daughter were moving to a bigger house, so they had their cabin listed for rent. Next thing I knew, I was signing my name on a year-long lease."

"That's serendipity, not magic."

"Semantics," Cullen countered.

"A year lease is a commitment."

"It has worked out fine."

"That's great, but I prefer renting month-to-month."

Of course she would. A month-to-month marriage would have been her first choice if that had been allowed. "You've always given yourself an out with everything you do."

Sarah stiffened. "I know better than to back myself into a corner."

She'd always been independent, but she sounded defensive as if the world were against her. He hadn't meant to attack her. "Someone might be there to help you escape."

"I'd rather not deal with the consequences if they're

not."

So jaded. And unlike her. He hoped their separation hadn't done this to Sarah. "People can surprise you."

"They usually do, but not in the way I expect."

Cullen wasn't sure what she meant, but the tip of a knife seemed to be pressing against his heart. Curiosity compelled him to ask the question. "Does that include me?"

"Yes."

The knife pierced his heart.

Her answer shouldn't have surprised him. She was impulsive and impatient with a tendency to erupt like the volcanoes she loved so much. He'd done his best to take care of her when they were married, but she'd pushed him away. He'd tried to make her happy, but she never seemed happy enough.

A lot like Blaine.

Cullen's jaw tightened to the point of aching. "Care to elaborate?"

"You've been great about my accident." Gratitude shone in her gaze. "I wasn't expecting that."

The tension in his jaw eased. "Couples in our situation can be friendly to each other."

She nodded. "Especially when divorce is what we both want."

The knife dug deeper. "It is."

A cheery love song played on the radio. The upbeat tempo was the antithesis of the growing tension between them. He fought the urge to press the power switch, wanting the music to stop.

"I'm glad you found the place you belong," Sarah said finally.

"Hood Hamlet is the best thing that's happened to me in a long time." He remembered the list he'd put together of places they could live after he finished his residency. Portland had been near the top because of the Cascades Volcano Observatory in nearby Vancouver, Washington, but he'd never considered Mount Hood. And he wouldn't have if they'd stayed together. "The only drawback is everyone wants to know everybody's business."

She clucked her tongue. "Typical small town."

"I sometimes forget how small."

She glanced his way. "Does that mean people are going to be talking about us?"

He took a deep breath and exhaled slowly. "They already are."

"Why is that?"

Cullen shouldn't have said anything. His stomach roiled.

"Tell me why."

His palms sweated. He wiped one on his jeans. "No one in Hood Hamlet knew I was married until your accident."

Her mouth gaped. She closed it. "Why didn't you tell them?"

He didn't want to admit he'd been nursing a wound so deep when he arrived in town he wasn't sure he would recover. But he had. And he'd been doing fine until she'd crashed into his world. "You were no longer a part of my life. I could start over in Hood Hamlet with a clean slate once the divorce was finalized."

The color drained from her face. Hurt flashed in her eyes. "You pretended to be single."

Her tone and stiff posture put him on the defensive. "Not intentionally."

She angled her shoulders toward the window.

"Hey, I'm not the bad guy here." He lowered his voice. "Don't forget you're the one who brought up a divorce."

"True, but you agreed," she countered. "And I didn't move to a new town and act like I was single."

"I haven't acted that way, either."

She stared at her cast with a downtrodden expression. "Sure you haven't."

"It's the truth." Her reaction surprised him. They'd been separated. Hadn't seen each other for almost a year. Divorce was a mere formality. "What were people supposed to think? I moved to Hood Hamlet alone. I wasn't wearing a wedding band. No one asked if I'd been married, so I saw no reason to tell them."

Sarah grasped her milkshake so hard she put a dent in the cup. "If they had asked?"

Not carrying around the baggage of a failed marriage had helped him move on. He'd never expected anyone, including Sarah, to find out. But by trying to make things easier on himself over this past year, he'd made them harder now. For Sarah, too. "I would have told the truth."

She bit her lower lip. "No wonder people are talking."

"Friends were with me when you were in ICU. They had questions."

She lifted her chin. "What do your friends know about our situation?"

"Not much."

"Cullen…"

She sounded more annoyed than hurt. But he wouldn't call that progress. "They know we've been separated for over a year but are together now."

She drew back with alarm. "Together?"

"For now."

Her mouth twisted.

"While you recover," he clarified.

"Well, I hope it won't take me long to get better so you can make your fresh start in Hood Hamlet and I can get back to Mount Baker."

At least they agreed on something. "Me, too. Except you can't rush the healing process. If you focus on one day at a time, you'll get to where you're supposed to be."

And so would he.

Then they could both get on with their separate lives.

Cullen couldn't wait for that to happen because spending time with Sarah was already harder on his heart than he'd anticipated. He had no idea how he'd feel after weeks, maybe months, of being together.

HIS SECOND CHANCE

Chapter Six

Sarah couldn't wait to arrive in Hood Hamlet. The drive had been uncomfortable and painful to her injuries but also to her heart. She couldn't change what had happened with Cullen. Over the past year, she'd analyzed every detail of their whirlwind romance, their year of marriage, her bringing up divorce, and their resulting separation. She had regrets over her actions, but she could only learn from her mistakes and move forward with her life. Cullen seemed to have done that. Seeing how he'd moved on twisted her insides.

She stared out the window.

The highway snaked up Mount Hood, giving panoramic views of the tree-covered mountainside. The dark green of the pines contrasted with the cornflower-blue sky. Breathtaking.

Still, not even the lovely landscape could replace Cullen's image in her mind.

He'd shaved, removing the sexy stubble from his

face. But he was still hot with the strong profile she knew by heart, warm blue eyes fringed by thick dark lashes that danced with laughter, and lush lips perfect for kisses.

Had been perfect.

Past tense.

A ballad played on the radio. The lyrics spoke of heartbreak and loneliness, two things she was familiar with.

Don't go there.

She and Cullen were better off apart. He'd found where he belonged—Hood Hamlet. She'd never had that, not even when they'd lived together. Once she finished her postdoc, she would keep looking until she found the haven she'd been searching for her whole life.

After a childhood of being shuttled between parents and stepparents as if she were a smelly dog no one wanted, she didn't need much. Nothing big and fancy, just a small place where she belonged and mattered.

Where she was loved.

She'd thought she found that with Cullen, but after a few months of marriage, she'd recognized the familiar signs from her childhood. She was older and wiser and knew what was going to happen. Only that time, she didn't have to wait to be abandoned. She'd been the one to end things before that happened.

Cullen touched her forearm. "Sarah…"

She jumped. The seat belt kept her in place, but her cast hit the door with a thud.

"You okay?" he asked.

Anxiety rose like the pressure building inside Yellowstone's Old Faithful. Sarah couldn't afford to erupt. She swallowed around the caldera-sized lump in her throat. The stronger she appeared, the more in control, the sooner she could return to Bellingham and work. She nodded, afraid her voice might quiver like her insides.

"We're coming into Hood Hamlet," he said.

He flicked on the blinker. The traffic heading west slowed. He turned onto a wide street. A gas station and convenience store sat on one corner, and trees lined the other side of the road, the treetops glistening in the sun. A short distance away, the peaks of roofs appeared.

She didn't believe in magic, but anticipation built over seeing this town Cullen called home.

The truck rounded a curve. Hood Hamlet came into view.

Surprise washed over her. The town was lovely. Picture-book perfect. Sarah could almost imagine herself in the Swiss Alps, not the Cascades, due to the architecture of the buildings.

"Welcome to Hood Hamlet." Cullen's voice held a note of reverence she understood now. No wonder he wanted to live here.

An Alpine inn resembled a life-sized four-story gingerbread house. A vacancy sign out front swayed from a wooden post. Flowers bloomed in planters hung beneath each of the wood-paned windows and from baskets fastened on wood rafters. "It's so quaint."

They approached a busier part of the street. He slowed the truck. "This is Main Street."

A row of shops and restaurants had a covered wooden sidewalk. People popped in and out of stores. A woman with three children waved at Cullen.

He returned the gesture with a smile. "That's Hannah Willingham with her kids, Kendall, Austin, and Tyler. Her husband, Garrett, is a CPA and OMSAR's treasurer."

A feeling of warmth settled at the center of Sarah's chest. "*Charming* describes Hood Hamlet perfectly."

"You should see the place at Christmastime. The town goes all out."

Hood Hamlet was made for the holidays with its mountain setting and pine trees. No doubt there'd be ample snow. She would love to see it in person. Too bad she would be long gone by then. "It must be wonderful."

"A winter wonderland." Cullen's face brightened. "There's an annual tree-lighting ceremony after Thanksgiving. The entire town attends no matter the weather. Wreaths and garland are hung across Main Street."

It sounded inviting and special. Her Christmases had never been like that. No holiday had been. "Is Easter a big deal in Hood Hamlet, too?"

"The town holds an annual egg hunt. It's low-key. Nothing like the shindig my mom and sisters put on. They could teach the Easter Bunny a thing or two," he joked.

Sarah found nothing humorous about it. Her hands balled. "Easter at your parents' house was like stepping into the middle of a magazine spread or home-decorating show."

"Holidays are big deals to my family."

No kidding.

"Watching your mom and sisters was exhausting." Easter with Cullen and his family had shown Sarah how different their childhoods and lives had been. Her parents didn't do much for the holidays. Meals, special occasion or not, were eaten in front of the television or skipped altogether. She'd planned a wedding that had never happened, but she didn't know how to cook for a huge crowd or be a proper hostess. "I tried to help, but I only slowed them down."

"Yeah, they go all out," he agreed. "I love it."

Cullen confirmed what Sarah had realized when they'd been together. She would never be able to pass muster with the Grays. Her shoulders sagged. The pain shooting down her right arm matched the hurt in her heart. She forced herself to sit straight.

"Holidays are more down to earth in Hood Hamlet but nice with many town traditions," he continued. "Santa and the Easter Bunny have been known to show up on Main Street to have their picture taken with kids and pets."

Pets? He'd never talked about animals before. "Do you have a pet?"

"No, but if I wasn't gone for so long when I work, I

might consider getting one."

"I thought you didn't like dogs and cats."

"I like them, but my dad's allergic," Cullen said. "One of the guys on the rescue unit has a Siberian husky named Denali. She's a cool dog."

"Get a cat. They're independent. A good pet for someone who is away a lot. Especially if you have two. That's what my boss, Tucker, says."

"I don't know if I'm a cat person. I'd want a pet that cares if I'm around or not."

She knew the feeling. "Cats care, but they don't show it."

"Then what's the use of having one?"

Sarah could have asked him the same question about having a wife. His serious nature and stability had appealed to her when they'd first met. He'd been the exact opposite of the other men in her life, the same ones who had disappointed and hurt her. But after they'd married, she'd realized the traits that initially appealed to her kept him from being spontaneous or showing emotion, leaving her feeling isolated and alone, like when she'd been a kid.

The one emotion he'd had no difficulty expressing was desire. No issues in that department. A heated flush rushed through her along with memories she'd rather forget. "You're better off without a pet."

Cullen turned onto a narrow street that wound its way through trees. Homes and cabins were interspersed among the pines.

"This is convenient to Main Street," she said.

"Especially to the brewpub."

Cullen's former mountain-rescue unit in Seattle went out for beers after missions, but callouts hadn't been weekly occurrences. She couldn't imagine rescues were that frequent on Mount Hood. He must enjoy going out with his friends.

No doubt women were involved.

Her left hand balled into a fist.

She flexed her fingers. "That must come in handy on Friday and Saturday nights."

"Very handy."

The thought of Cullen with another woman sent a shudder through Sarah. "Who do you go to the brewpub with?"

"Mostly OMSAR members and a few firefighters."

"Nice guys?"

"Yes, but not all are men."

Her shoulders tensed. This was none of her business. Some people dated before a divorce was finalized. She shouldn't care or be upset over what Cullen did.

A quarter mile down the road, he pulled into the driveway in front of a small, single-story cabin. "This is it."

Sarah stared in disbelief. She'd been expecting an A-frame, not something that belonged in a storybook. The log cabin was delightful, with wood beams and small-paned windows. A planter containing colorful flowers sat next to the front door. "It's adorable. I half expect to see

Snow White appear, followed by the seven dwarfs."

He stopped the truck and set the parking brake. "I suppose the place has a certain amount of curb appeal, but I wouldn't go that far."

"You have to admit it's cute."

He pulled the keys out of the ignition. "The house suits my purpose."

She opened the passenger door. "I can't wait to see the inside."

"Stay there." Cullen exited, crossed in front of the truck, and stood next to her. He extended his arm. "I'll help you."

She'd appreciated his manners the first time they met. Gentlemanly behavior wasn't something she was used to. It made her feel special. Ignoring her soreness, she reached for his hand. "Thanks."

"Go slowly." He wrapped his hand around her waist. "I'll get the luggage once you're settled."

She wasn't about to argue. Not when the warmth of his skin sent heat rushing through her veins. All she had to do was make it to the front door and inside the cabin. Then she could let go and catch her breath.

Cullen escorted her as if she were as delicate as a snowflake. She took cautious steps, fighting the urge to hurry so he wouldn't keep touching her. The scent of him embraced her. Every point of contact was sweet torture. Relief nearly knocked her over when she reached the porch step.

He squeezed her hand. "Careful."

Yes, she needed to be careful around Cullen. Reactions to him could bring disaster down on her already hurting head.

Reaching around her, he unlocked the door. A feeling of déjà vu washed over her. When they'd arrived in Seattle after eloping, Cullen had taken her to his apartment. After sweeping her up into his arms, he'd carried her over the threshold. The romantic gesture had sent her heart singing. Reassured her getting married hadn't been a mistake.

"It's a good thing Snow White and her crew aren't here, or this place would be too crowded." He pushed open the door with his foot. "Go on in."

No romance today.

But that was what she'd wanted.

Still, Sarah hated the twinge of disappointment arcing through her. After releasing his hand, she stepped through the doorway.

The decor was comfortable and inviting. The kitchen was small but functional, with stainless-steel appliances and a tiled island with a breakfast bar. The bar stools matched the pine table and six chairs in the dining room that separated the kitchen from the living room. "Nice place."

A river rock fireplace with a wood mantel on the far wall drew her attention. She imagined a crackling fire would be nice when the temperature dropped. A large television was tucked into the space above the fireplace.

An overstuffed leather couch was positioned in front of the fireplace/TV. The perfect place to relax after a long day. Log-pole coffee and end tables, as well as photographs and artwork, added a touch of the outdoors to the rustic yet welcoming decor. "You got new furniture."

He closed the door behind him. "I rented this place furnished."

"Did you put your stuff in storage?"

"I sold it."

She glanced around. Nothing was familiar. "Everything?"

"Most of it was castoffs from friends and family. No sense dragging that old stuff here with me."

Sarah ignored a flash of hurt. She'd given him a framed photograph from Red Rocks on their first wedding anniversary. And then she remembered. "A fresh start."

"Yes."

"Nice cabin." Much nicer than any place she'd ever lived, including the apartment they'd shared. "I see why you signed a year lease."

"I'm comfortable here."

If she'd ever wondered if Cullen needed her, Sarah had her answer. He didn't. He had a nice place to live, friends, and a good job. His life was complete without her.

Too bad she couldn't say the same thing about her

life without him.

Maybe she needed to work harder on that.

After she recovered, she would.

Chapter Seven

"Something smells good."

Sarah's voice sent a thunderbolt of awareness through Cullen, jolting him to reality. For the past two hours, he'd relished the solitude of the cabin, pretending she wasn't asleep in the guest bedroom.

He placed the hot pad on the counter. "Dinner."

She stood where the hallway ended and the living room began with bare feet and tangled hair, sleep-rumpled and sexy. "I didn't expect to wake up to dinner cooking."

He glimpsed ivory skin where the hem of her T-shirt bunched above her waistband. Her baggy sweatpants, a pair of his because her jeans were too uncomfortable to wear due to her injuries, rode low on her hips even though the drawstring was pulled tight.

Cullen focused on her face. Still roughed-up after the accident, but pretty nonetheless. "You took a long nap."

"The mattress at the hospital was as hard as a slab of

granite. Yours is like sleeping on a cloud."

Too bad she was more devilish than angelic. "I told you this place would be better than a SNF."

"Yes, you did."

But having her here would be difficult for him. His gaze strayed to the enticing band of bare skin at her waist. The hint of flesh tantalized, reminding him of what would never be his again.

He jammed a spoon into the saucepan of refried beans and stirred.

"I'm glad I listened," she said.

He realized she was wearing the same clothes as earlier. They weren't dirty but something that fit better might be more comfortable. "Do you want to change into pajamas?"

Shrugging her left shoulder, she studied a photograph of Illumination Rock hanging on the wall.

His stomach dropped. "You can't undress yourself."

The thought of helping her do that hadn't crossed his mind. He'd been thinking about his needs, not hers.

"I probably could if I tried." Sarah didn't sound upset, more resigned. "But I didn't think about changing when we arrived. I hit the mattress and was out."

Cullen felt like a jerk. He should have checked on her more carefully. But he hadn't wanted to get too close after the drive.

Good work, Dr. Gray.

The sound of Blaine's voice mocking Cullen, blaming him with a growing list of transgressions, was almost too much for him to take. He lowered the temperature on the beans before checking the Spanish rice.

He should have done more for Sarah, except he'd needed a break. He might be a physician, but he was still a man. One who hadn't kissed or touched a woman since he'd moved out of their apartment. Despite their marriage falling apart and the hard feelings that brought with it, undressing Sarah would mean taking a cold shower after he finished.

Cullen would have to get past that. He was responsible for her well-being. "I'll help you after…"

Sarah's face paled.

His stomach clenched. *What the—*

She swayed unsteadily.

Adrenaline surged. Cullen ran.

She slumped against the wall.

He wrapped his arms around her before she crumpled to the ground like a house of cards. "I've got you."

Her warmth, softness, and smell were sweet ambrosia. Blood rushed through his veins. He recalled parts of the anatomy…in Latin. Though organic chemistry equations might work better to distract him.

"Thanks." Her breath caressed his neck, sending pleasurable sensations through him. "I was dizzy. I must have gotten out of bed too fast."

He should have been paying closer attention to her health, not other parts of her. "You've had a long day.

It's been a while since you ate."

"The milkshake—"

"Food."

She straightened. "I feel better now."

"Good, but let's not take any chances." He swept her into his arms, ignoring her sharp inhalation and how good holding her felt. "I don't want you to fall."

As if concern explained the acceleration of his pulse or his breathlessness.

Wariness clouded her gaze. "I don't want you to strain your back."

"Thanks for the concern, but you barely weigh anything." Sarah had always been fit but never this thin. He carried her to the couch. "We'll have to put some meat on you."

Sarah frowned. "That's not what a woman wants to hear."

"Men like women with curves. Gives them something to hold on to."

Awareness flickered in her eyes. Sarah parted her lips.

All he had to do was lower his mouth to hers and…

"Some men," she said.

If he'd had a thermometer under his tongue, the mercury would have shot out the end and made a real mess. "This man."

Tension sizzled in the air. The physical chemistry between them remained strong. If the past sixty seconds were anything to go by, still highly combustible.

Fighting the urge to get away from her before his control slipped any further, he placed her gently on the couch. "Rest while I finish getting dinner ready."

He strode to the kitchen with one purpose in mind—putting distance between him and Sarah, even if the space was less than twelve feet. Attraction or not, he had to be more careful. She was injured and his soon-to-be ex-wife.

Cullen checked the beans and the rice. He glanced at the clock on the microwave. "Time for your meds."

"I'd rather not take them." The couch hid all but the top of her head. "They make me loopy."

"Staying ahead of the pain is important."

"I'm ahead of it."

Not for long. Her voice sounded strained.

He filled a glass with water and dispensed her pills. "This isn't up for negotiation."

She poked up her head. "Whatever you're cooking smells so good."

"Enchiladas."

"One of my favorites."

Changing the subject wasn't like Sarah. She must not feel well. He carried the water and medicine to her. "Here you go."

She stared at the capsules as if they were poison. "Your patients must call you Dr. Hardnose."

He handed her the medication. "They might but not to my face. Well, except you."

"I'm not your patient." She shot him a chilly glance, popped the pills into her mouth, and drank the water.

"Satisfied?"

"Very. It's not often you do what you're told."

"I only took the pills because you made dinner."

"Then it's a good thing I didn't tell you someone else made the meal," he said with an ornery grin.

"Who?"

"Carly Porter." He placed Sarah's water glass on the coffee table. "She stopped by while you were sleeping."

A thoughtful expression crossed Sarah's face. "That sure is nice of Carly."

Sarah's voice sounded tight, almost on edge. She needed those pills. "Carly and her husband are good people. Jake's the one who owns the brewpub, and they rented this cabin to me."

A corner of Sarah's mouth curved upward. "Oh, you mentioned them during the drive."

The timer on the oven dinged.

"Dinner's ready," Cullen announced. "You can eat on the couch."

"I've been eating in bed. I'd rather sit at the table, if that's okay?"

His stomach twisted. This would be their first meal together since she'd brought up divorce.

She touched her cast. "If you'd rather I eat here—"

"The table works." He was being stupid. Just because the last time had ended badly didn't mean this dinner would. A few minutes ago, he'd wanted to kiss her. No matter how he viewed this situation, an epic fail seemed imminent. "Give me a sec."

As Cullen set the table, utensils clattered against the plates. His hands shook. He wasn't sure what had gotten into him, but he felt clumsy, a way he wasn't used to feeling.

He placed the hot casserole dish, bowls of rice and refried beans, and a bottle of sparkling apple cider on the table, leaving the six-pack of Hood Hamlet Brewing Company's Hogsback Ale, courtesy of Jake, in the refrigerator. Cullen needed his wits about him with Sarah here. "Dinner's ready."

He helped her up from the couch, conscious of her every movement and aware of each brush of his skin sparking against hers.

She squeezed his hand. "Thanks."

A lump formed in his throat. He grumbled, "You're welcome," before escorting her to the table. Keeping his arm around her in case she became lightheaded—yeah, that was the reason, all right—he pulled out a chair and helped her sit. His hand lingered on her.

Sarah placed her napkin in her lap. "The food looks delicious."

Her lips sure did.

What was he doing?

Sarah had an excuse for acting loopy. Cullen didn't. He dropped his hand to his side.

"I can't believe someone made you dinner." She sounded amazed.

After he settled in the seat across from her, he dished up chicken enchiladas smothered in a green tomatillo sauce. "Carly and Jake did this for you, too."

"No one's ever done something like this for me."

He dropped a spoonful of refried beans onto her plate and then one on his. "People are helpful in Hood Hamlet."

She motioned to the serving spoon in his hand. "You included."

Cullen added a scoop of the rice. "You'll serve yourself soon enough."

Sarah's shoulders drooped as if someone had let the air out of her. "I'd make a big mess right now, and you'd have to clean up after me."

That was what she'd done with the divorce. Brought it up and then made him deal with it.

He took a sip of the sparkling cider. The sweetness did nothing to alter the bitter taste in his mouth. Maybe a beer wasn't such a bad idea. Just one. He never had more than that with dinner, anyway.

"You're smart for serving tonight," she continued.

A smart man would never have allowed his heart to overrule logic so he ended up marrying a total stranger in Las Vegas. "Just trying to be helpful."

"I…appreciate it."

As they ate, Cullen wondered if she did. She hadn't appreciated what he'd done when they were together.

Bubbles rose in his glass, making him think of champagne. Marriage was like champagne bubbles, first rising in pairs, then groups of three, then individually. He was thankful he and Sarah had skipped the middle part by not having a baby right away. A divorce was bad enough without having to deal with a custody battle. "It's a practical decision. I don't have time for extra chores tonight. I work the third shift at the hospital tomorrow, and I need to get back into my routine."

Maybe being in his own bed would let him get some much-needed rest. He hoped so.

She studied him over the rim of her glass. "Who will be my nursemaid?"

"I found the perfect babysitter."

Sarah stuck her tongue out at him.

That was more like it. He grinned. "We could go with *nanny* if you prefer."

She waved her cast in the air. "I bet this thing could do some damage."

"To yourself most definitely."

"Very funny." She feigned annoyance, but laughter danced in her eyes. "So who's stuck here with me first?"

"Leanne Thomas," Cullen said. "I know her from OMSAR. She's also a paramedic."

"Sounds capable."

"I'd trust her with my life. In fact, I have," he admitted. "You'll be in good hands.

"I'm in good hands now."

He appreciated the compliment, but he'd fallen down on the job this afternoon. "I'm trying to do my best."

"You are," she agreed. "I'm not sure how I'll ever repay you."

"You don't have to." That was the truth. He didn't want anything from her. Well, except to finalize their divorce. "I remember what it was like."

Wrinkles formed on her forehead. "Remember what?"

"To have a broken arm."

She leaned over the table. "When did you break your arm?"

"I was eleven." He took another enchilada from the pan. "Want more?"

"No, thanks." Sarah stared at him. "I had no idea about your arm. How did you break it?"

"A soccer tournament. This big kid shoved me out of bounds after I scored a goal. I landed wrong. Ended up fracturing my arm in two places."

"Ouch."

"That's all I could say in between grimacing and crying."

She drew away as if horrified. "You cry?"

"Past tense. I was eleven."

"I'm teasing." She stared at her plate. "Nothing wrong with crying, no matter what your age."

"Only if you're an emotional, overwrought sissy."

Her gaze jerked to his. "Wouldn't want someone to take away your man card."

He nodded once. Even though she was joking, he'd cried more than he wanted to admit after they split.

She sipped her cider. "Tell me more about your broken arm."

Cullen patted his mouth with a napkin. "Not much more to tell. It happened in early July, so I spent the rest of my summer in a cast. It sucked."

"You do know how I feel."

He nodded. "I couldn't swim or go in the sprinklers. I wasn't allowed to ride my bike or skateboard. No going on rides at the county fair, either. Casts weren't allowed."

"That must have been the worst summer of your life."

Nope. That was a toss-up between last summer when he was trying to get over her and the summer after his brother died. Her rejection, however, had hurt more than his arm fracture. "It wasn't fun, but I survived. So will you."

She flinched.

Of course she did.

His harsh tone contained not an ounce of sympathy or compassion.

"I'm sorry." Being with Sarah brought out strong feelings and emotions he'd rather forget existed. "That was rude of me."

"Don't worry about it." She took a breath before exhaling slowly, as if trying to figure out what she wanted to say. "It's been a long day, and you did all the driving."

That wasn't the reason for his behavior, but he took the out.

Forks scraped against plates. Glasses were raised and returned to the table. The lack of conversation only emphasized the awkwardness of the situation. But Cullen didn't know what to do about it. He'd never known what to do with Sarah except kiss her and take her to bed.

Not an option tonight or any time in the future.

Even if a part of him wished it were.

Chapter Eight

As Cullen loaded the dishwasher, Sarah sat at the table with a plate of cookies within arm's reach. Medication dulled the pain, but she felt loopy as if she'd drunk one beer too many. Maybe that was why dinner had seemed so weird. Forget walking on eggshells—the floor was covered in shattered glass and she kept stepping on the shards.

The uncomfortable silence reminded her of the unsettling quiet that had consumed their marriage. If Sarah could have made it to the guest bedroom on her own, she would have bolted after she'd finished eating. But since she couldn't, death by chocolate chips sounded like the best alternative.

She bit into a cookie. The sweet flavor exploded in her mouth. "These are great."

Cullen glanced over his shoulder. "Carly is known for her baking skills."

"I can see why." Sarah had been surprised about his

broken arm. She wondered what else she didn't know about him. They'd communicated in bed, but that hadn't been enough after a while.

She reached for the plate. "I'm going to have another."

"Save me one."

Her hand hovered above the plate. "There are over a dozen."

Cullen glanced over his shoulder. Amusement—at least that was what she hoped it was—flashed in his eyes. "I know how much you love cookies."

"You gave me a cookie bouquet for my birthday." That had been five months into their marriage. He'd also covered their bed with rose petals. A romantic gesture when romance had been nonexistent. "They were tasty."

"I never got one."

"That's because you ran off to your shift at the hospital, and I didn't hear from you for two days."

Cullen gave her one of those you-have-to-be-kidding looks. "I had to work."

By the time he'd returned home, the cookies had been eaten and the rose petals had wilted. "You never called or texted. Not even during breaks."

He tugged at his collar. "I need to concentrate when I'm at the hospital. Lives are at stake. I can't afford to be distracted."

Her muscles bunched, which only made her body hurt more. He had never owned up to his behavior in the past. Why had she expected anything different now? Best to forget everything that had happened. Good or bad.

She pushed the plate away. "Help yourself. You'll have to roll me to my room if I eat another."

"Roll you, carry you." He bent to put something in the dishwasher. "Not much difference."

Maybe not for him.

A wave of helplessness washed over Sarah, threatening to drown her. She hated not being able to do anything for herself. She hated being at someone else's mercy. She hated relying on anybody.

Oh-so-familiar disappointment pressed down on her. She had finally been getting everything on track when life threw a rock at her—literally. She didn't want to have to depend on Cullen. She didn't want to end up needing him.

The tight ball of emotion in her belly unraveled like yarn, sending pent-up feelings rolling through her.

She couldn't unsnap her bra or wear pants that zipped or be the kind of wife a man would love forever.

Tears stung her eyes.

Oh, no. Sarah didn't want him to see her upset. She was independent and strong, not needy and emotional. Except she wanted to cry. Needed to.

She blinked. Tilted her head up. Drops still fell. She dabbed at the tears with the napkin.

Time to get out of here.

Without Cullen's help.

Using her good hand, she pushed against the table. Mantling had always been a favorite climbing move, but

97

this took more effort than she was used to exerting. Her muscles protested. Her abdomen ached. Still she managed to stand, scooting the chair back in the process.

Silverware clattered into the sink. Cullen rushed to her side. "What are you doing?"

"I don't need to be rolled or carried." Her voice cracked. "I can do it myself."

Except she couldn't. All she wanted to do was sit. Pride kept her standing.

"I was kidding." He sounded annoyed, not amused. "Like old times."

Sarah raised her chin, but that didn't make up the difference in height. She reminded herself they were equals in every other way. At least, she liked to think so. "The old times weren't that great."

He flinched. "They weren't that bad."

She shrugged, hoping the gesture hid her hurt. "I'm used to taking care of myself. I can do this."

But if she didn't move, she would be flat on her bottom in about ten seconds.

"Tomorrow"—he scooped her into his arms—"not tonight. Time to get you into your pajamas and into bed."

Cradled against his strong, wide chest, she struggled to breathe. Her muscles tensed. Her senses reeled.

What was happening to her?

Sarah wanted to be strong, but she also wanted to collapse against him and forget everything that had happened in the past and whatever would happen in the future.

But that wouldn't be a smart move.

Not when the feel of his heartbeat sent hers into a frenetic rhythm. Or when the musky scent of him made her want to take another sniff.

"You don't have to do this." She tried to keep the panic out of her voice. "I'm okay."

Or would be once she was out of his arms and into bed.

Alone.

With the door locked.

As Sarah focused on his lips, heat exploded inside her. She looked away.

"You're not okay." He carried her down the hallway. "I don't need a medical degree to see you're exhausted."

She opened her mouth to deny it but couldn't. "I'll feel better in the morning."

"I'd rather you feel better now."

Maybe if she had a good cry or if he kissed her…

He kicked open the bathroom door with his foot, flipped on the light with his elbow, and set her on her feet, keeping his hands on her. "Let's get you ready for bed."

Her heart beat a rapid tattoo. She leaned against the counter for support. "My toiletry kit is in my suitcase."

A coworker had packed a bag for Sarah and dropped it off at the hospital yesterday.

Cullen opened a drawer, removed a new toothbrush, and unwrapped the plastic covering. "Use this."

"You have spare toothbrushes?"

"People sack out here if they don't want to drive home."

People? Or women? Sarah didn't want to know.

He squirted toothpaste on it. "Here you go."

She took the toothbrush in her usable hand.

What was going on? One minute, he seemed upset at her. The next, he was concerned. The flip-flopping made her dizzy. Or maybe the pain medication was the reason. That could explain her crying.

"I'll brush your teeth for you," he said.

She shoved the toothbrush into her mouth. "Got it."

"Be right back."

Sarah took advantage of the moment of privacy, awkwardly brushing her teeth, washing her face, and combing the tangles out of her hair. The effort and whatever pills she'd swallowed wiped her out. Made her dizzy. She released a frustrated breath.

Cullen stood in the doorway. "Finished?"

Sarah nodded. He followed her to the guest room.

A queen-sized bed with a headboard made of twigs dominated the room. He'd straightened the bedding and pulled back the covers, something he'd done for her when he worked graveyard shifts. Her chest tightened with memories and regrets.

A full glass of water sat on the knotty pine nightstand. A cookie lay on a paper towel. Tears welled. "I don't deserve—"

He placed his finger at her lips. "Shh."

The slight touch sent chills down her spine. She

couldn't have said anything if she'd wanted to.

Cullen tucked a strand of hair behind her ear. "I didn't take good care of you earlier."

Her heart stilled. She knew he meant today, but a part of her wished he'd meant during their marriage.

"I'm making up for this afternoon," he continued.

Sarah released the breath she hadn't realized she was holding. Her disappointment was a not-so-subtle reminder of how stupid she became around Cullen. "You're not my manservant."

Mischief did the tango in his eyes. "I could be if that's what you wanted."

She wanted…him.

No, that was the pain medication talking. More tears welled. She wiped her face.

He embraced her. "It's going to be okay."

Not with her pressed against his broad, muscular chest and her heart thudding. "I'm sorry. I'm loopy."

"You're cute when you're loopy."

He pulled her closer and she sank against him, too tired to keep fighting herself. He felt so good. Warm. And strong. "You're cute when I'm loopy."

Cullen laughed. The deep sound was the best medicine of all. "Where are your pajamas?"

"In my suitcase."

"Sit."

She sat on the bed while he unzipped her luggage.

He removed a floral-printed nightshirt. "This work?"

"Yes."

Cullen placed it on the bed. He pulled on her bra band through her T-shirt. The strap unhooked.

Heat rushed up her neck. "You've, um, always been good at that."

"A little rusty, but it's like riding a bike."

Her pulse quickened. "I haven't ridden in a while."

Too long. She missed it. Missed him.

No, she missed the idea of him, of what they could have had together if fairy tales existed. This—what was happening right now—wasn't real.

He brushed his hand over her hair. "You can always hop back on."

Sarah's mouth went dry. She opened her mouth to speak, but nothing came out.

Cullen held onto the hem of her shirt. "Let's get this off you."

Let's not. She crossed her arm and her cast in front of her chest. "I want to see if I can do it."

"Sure."

She waited for him to turn around. He didn't. Frustration grew. "Maybe you could face the other way."

He turned toward the wall.

Self-preservation helped her undress and put on the nightshirt. Thank goodness she'd taken the pain pills, or she'd be unable to function. "You can turn around."

As soon as he did, his gaze raked over her. "I'm impressed."

She was about to fall asleep. "Thanks."

"I'll untie your sweats."

As he pushed up her nightshirt, his hand brushed her stomach. Sparks flew outward from where he'd touched her. So not good.

He untied the drawstring and then gently pushed the oversized sweats past her hips, thighs, and then calves. "Step out."

She did.

"Time for bed."

Before Sarah could blink, she was horizontal with her head against the pillow. She had no idea how he'd managed to get her in this position so effortlessly, but she was beyond the point of caring.

Cullen pulled the sheet and comforter over her.

"You don't have to do this," she said quietly.

He brushed his lips across her forehead with a featherlight kiss. "It's been a long day. The least I can do is tuck you in."

Emotion overflowed from her heart. She felt special.

He touched the top of her head. "Sweet dreams, Lavagirl."

Who needed dreams? Reality was pretty sweet right now. Sarah wanted him to stay, to hold her, until she fell asleep.

"Thank you, Dr. Gray." She felt dreamy and a tad wistful. "For everything."

"I'm right across the hall if you need anything."

He flicked off the light, exited the room, and closed the door behind him.

And then it hit her.

She and Cullen had never spent a night in the same place without sleeping in the same bed. Not until tonight. Her heart panged.

A door closed out in the hallway. Water sounded. The shower.

Well, there was always a first time. Sarah touched the empty space next to her. But she had to admit she'd rather there wasn't.

Even if she knew better.

Chapter Nine

Someone coughed.

Cullen bolted upright from a dead sleep. He blinked, not quite sure what was going on. Rays of sunlight peeked around the edges of the window blinds. The digital clock on his nightstand read six forty-five.

Another cough.

Sarah.

Pulse pounding, he jumped out of bed, ran to her room, and flung open the door. She lay in bed. Her hair was a tangled mess. Her face, what he could see through her hair, was pale. "Sarah?"

"I coughed." Her voice sounded hoarse. "It hurts."

"I'm sure it does." He sat next to her. "Let me check your incision."

Her eyes widened with a hint of panic. "It was the cough."

He brushed the hair away from her face. His fingers touched her cheek. She didn't feel warm. "I want to make sure."

She pulled the blanket to her neck. "You don't have to go to all this trouble."

"It's no trouble." He understood Sarah's leeriness. Even after a cold shower, he'd wanted to sleep in here, to hold her, to breathe in her scent. Loneliness did strange things to a man. "If you were in a SNF, someone would check you."

"Yes, but not…"

"Me."

She nodded. "I'm sorry."

"Don't apologize."

Her fingers rubbed the edge of the blanket. "It's the situation. I'm not sure how to feel around you. Parts of last night were nice, then awkward, then nice again. So nice I hated sleeping alone."

A combination of relief and satisfaction radiated through him. He'd thought the same thing. He touched her shoulder.

Her muscles tensed beneath his hand.

"I get it," he admitted. "Having you here is…"

"Weird."

"Different," he said at the same time. "A little weird, too."

She blew out a puff of air. "Good. I mean, not that things are weird, but that I'm not alone or imagining things."

"You're not alone." He'd been imagining things about her all night. Unfortunately. Because those fantasies would never become reality. "We're adults. We can handle this."

"It's not like we have another choice."

If only… "It is what it is until you're ready to go to Bellingham."

"If things get too weird, we can talk it out."

She'd wanted to discuss everything. He hated doing that. He'd been talked out after his parents made him and his brother attend family therapy with them due to Blaine's addiction and then grief sessions for the three of them and his sisters following Blaine's death. The intense sessions helped, but they also frustrated Cullen because no amount of counseling or rehab had been able to help his brother kick his drug addiction.

Sarah stared expectantly at him.

"Sure, we can talk," Cullen relented. "May I please check your incision?"

She lowered the blanket. "It's not like you haven't seen this before."

He slowly raised the hem of her nightshirt over her thighs. The bruises were fading. He lifted the material higher, past her orange polka-dotted bikini panties that showed off the curve of her hip. Cullen had seen her before, but he willed his hand not to tremble. He continued to the large incision on her abdomen from her emergency splenectomy.

The area around the sutures wasn't any redder than it had been at the hospital. No drainage, either. He placed his fingertips on her stomach. Her skin wasn't hot but soft and smooth.

He dragged his hand away. "No drainage or rash. Are you hungry?"

She nodded.

"That's a good sign." He lowered the hem of her nightshirt until she was fully covered. "Has the pain lessened since the surgery?"

"Yes, until I coughed."

"Next time you have to cough, place a pillow over your incision. That should help." He stood. "Let's get you up and moving. That will ease some of the pain, too."

She scrunched her nose. "It's too early for you to be up if you have to work tonight."

Her concern brought a smile to his face. "I'll nap later."

"You're sure?"

"Positive." Cupping her elbow, he helped her out of bed. "Is it difficult to breathe?"

"Nope."

She sounded confident. Another good sign.

"Let's see how you feel walking."

She moved slowly and carefully, the way she should to make sure she didn't fall. "Being upright helps."

He noticed her long legs with the attractive curves of her calves and the slender slopes of her ankles. "You're doing great."

She headed out of the bedroom. "I must look frightening."

He followed her down the hall. "You look good for

someone recovering from a bad fall, broken bones, and surgery."

She glanced over her shoulder, her green eyes hopeful. "Any chance I could shower?"

An image of him taking off her panties flashed in his mind. He gave his head a mental shake. "Uh, sure. I'll have to wrap your cast."

"That's what the nurse did at the hospital." Sarah sounded relieved. "I may need you to pour the shampoo and conditioner for me."

Once upon a time, she would have asked him to wash her hair. "I can do that."

"Thanks."

"You're welcome." A good attitude would help her recovery. That meant getting along and playing nice. He was willing to do both. "Let's get you fed, then cleaned up."

Sarah stood in the bathroom wearing her orange robe with nothing underneath. She stared at the tile floor, not wanting to meet Cullen's watchful gaze. To keep the robe from slipping open, she tightened the belt around her waist as best she could with one hand.

Stupid given he was her husband and knew her body as well as she did, but a shyness overtook her. Needing his help so badly quadrupled her vulnerabilities.

His height and wide shoulders made the space feel cramped even though the bathroom was larger than the one at the hospital. He checked the plastic around her cast. "It should stay dry."

She studied the wrapping. "I think this would survive a swim."

Water from the shower splashed against the tub and curtain. "That's the plan."

"You always were a planner." Too bad he hadn't stuck to his plans instead of letting her derail them. That would have saved them both a lot of heartache. Well, at least her.

"I'm trying."

He wasn't the trying type, which meant he was probably being polite. "Have your life all figured out once again?"

"Pretty much. I made a few changes."

Like removing her from his future. She pinched the bridge of her nose, ignoring the hollow feeling inside her.

He checked the water temperature. "Ready?"

Not really. "Sure."

He pulled open the shower curtain. "There's a mat on the bottom of the tub, so you shouldn't slip, but be careful."

"Okay."

She waited for him to leave. He didn't.

"Aren't you getting in?" he asked.

Cullen stared at her as if she had something on her face. Leftover French toast, perhaps? She rubbed her hand over her mouth. "Are you staying in here?"

"Yes."

It was as simple and as complicated as that.

"I need to hand you the shampoo," he reminded her.

Oh, yeah. She'd forgotten about that. But still, she hesitated. "This is kind of awkward."

"Only if we make it awkward."

"I'm not trying to."

"Neither am I."

"But I'm the one who is naked under my robe."

"I can undress."

She shot him a squinty-eyed glare.

With a grin, he faced the door. "Better?"

"Yes, thank you." Mustering her courage with a deep breath wasn't going to work with her incision and ribs. Settling for a slight intake of air, she untied the belt, dropped her robe, and stepped inside the tub. She closed the shower curtain. "You can turn around now."

"Is the water the right temperature?"

Hot water poured over her. Steam rose toward the ceiling. She picked up a bar of soap. "Perfect."

"I remember you like it hot."

She remembered the showers they'd taken together. The soap slipped out of her hand and clattered to the tub.

"Sarah—"

"I dropped the soap," she said at the same time.

"Can you reach it?" he asked.

Bending hurt. But she wasn't about to ask him to get the soap for her. That would be way more awkward. "No, but it's okay. I mainly wanted to wash my hair."

"I've got the shampoo," he said. "Stick out your hand when you want some."

Once her hair was wet enough, she extended her arm. The cooler air temperature made her shiver. Goose bumps covered her exposed skin.

He poured a dollop of shampoo onto her palm. "Is that enough?"

"Yes."

Washing her hair was easier this time. "I'm getting the hang of using one hand."

"Just takes time."

Time she didn't have. For the past twenty-four hours, Cullen had occupied the majority of her thoughts. Not Mount Baker. Once she had work to distract her, everything would return to normal. She couldn't wait for that to happen. She rinsed the shampoo from her hair.

"Ready for the conditioner?"

"Please." She poked her fingers out, palm up.

"Need more?"

Yes, but not from him. He hadn't been able to give her what she needed. Nor could she do the same for him. That was why they were better off apart. Still, the thought made her heart hurt. Not a want-to-throw-herself-a-pity-party aching, but a too-bad-this-couldn't-have-worked pining. "I'm good."

And after she returned to the institute with her marriage behind her, everything else in her life would be good, too. Given how bad things had been, it sure couldn't get any worse.

Later that evening, the doorbell rang. Sarah remained on the couch while Cullen answered the door. Her babysitter for the night, Leanne Thomas, must have arrived.

Sarah couldn't wait for Cullen to go to work. A physical separation from him would be a relief, even though she'd spent most of her day in bed. But she'd been thinking about him constantly. The last place he belonged was on her mind. Well, actually in her heart was the last place, but that wasn't going to happen again.

A woman with shiny brown hair, an easy smile, and wearing a huge diamond engagement ring carried in a platter of mini red velvet cupcakes and a large shopping bag. She placed the two on the kitchen table before removing a green tote from her shoulder. "Hi, I'm Leanne."

"I'm Sarah." Cullen had called the paramedic and mountain-rescue volunteer tough as nails and described her as by the book, but Sarah didn't get that impression at all. "Nice to meet you."

"The pleasure is mine." Leanne glanced at Cullen, who was sticking a water bottle into his backpack. "Hope I'm not late."

"Right on time." He swung a strap over his shoulder. "Thanks for taking the overnight shift. There's a list of instructions on the breakfast bar. Sarah's meds are on the kitchen counter. She should rest as much as possible. Short walks are okay but not outside."

"Bummer. I thought we could take a midnight stroll around Mirror Lake," Leanne teased.

His gaze hardened. "You're kidding."

Sarah shook her head. He needed to lighten up and not take things so seriously.

Leanne's mouth quirked. "Give me a little credit."

"Just making sure." He glanced at Sarah before addressing Leanne. "Call me if you have any questions."

What? When had that changed? Sarah bit her lower lip. When they were together, he hadn't wanted her to call him at work no matter what was going on. When she had left a message, he'd never gotten in touch. Most of the times she'd tried calling had been because she missed him and wanted to hear his voice, but he hadn't cared.

"I'm sure Sarah can answer any questions I might have," Leanne replied in a matter-of-fact tone.

"Definitely." Sarah appreciated how direct Leanne was. "I haven't seen Cullen's instructions, but my doctor's orders are to take my medication. Sleep. Rest. Sleep some more. Rest some more."

Leanne frowned. "Sounds boring."

"It is," Sarah agreed. "One day here, and I'm a couch potato."

Cullen's lip curled. "Resting is important if you want to recover."

"True, but you can still do stuff while you take it

easy," Leanne said. "I'll have to see what I can come up with."

"Thomas." Cullen's voice contained a clear warning.

"Relax, Doc." Leanne's stern reply made Sarah bite back a giggle. "Sarah will be fine. Get going before we throw you out."

He raised his hands in mock surrender. "I'm going."

As soon as the door closed, Leanne sat on the couch. "I'm sorry about your fall."

"Thanks. I was at the wrong place at the wrong time."

"Well, you're in the right place now. Hood Hamlet will be good for you. It won't be long until you're exploring Main Street."

"I can't wait."

Leanne motioned to the bag she'd brought. "I have pants that should be more comfortable for you to wear."

Sarah stared in disbelief. "For me?"

Leanne nodded. "Sweats, yoga pants, leggings. Some are for lounging around the house, but others you can wear to doctor's appointments or when you're ready to get out and about."

"That's so sweet of you." Sarah was stunned a stranger would do that for her. "Thanks."

"Thank Cullen."

Wait, what? Sarah's gaze bounced from the bag to Leanne. "Cullen asked you to do this?"

The paramedic's eyes twinkled. "This was his idea. He said between your abdominal surgery and broken arm, jeans won't work and asked if I could go shopping. He told me your sizes. Said to get comfy pants with no buttons or zippers."

"I…" Sarah was speechless. She'd never expected him to do something so thoughtful. "I appreciate you doing that for him and me."

"Happy to help. You'll find most people in Hood Hamlet are willing to lend a hand." As she removed the items from the bag and stacked them on the table, colorful prisms of light reflected off Leanne's diamond ring and danced around the living room. After she finished, she stared lovingly at her ring.

Sarah had worn a diamond like that once but not with Cullen. They'd picked plain gold bands at the wedding chapel. "Congratulations on your engagement."

Leanne beamed. "Thanks. I still can't believe I'm getting married."

"Have you set a wedding date?"

She nodded. "The Saturday before Christmas. We hadn't been together long when Christian, my fiancé, proposed on Christmas Day so we thought a year engagement sounded good."

Very good. A year was long enough to get to know someone, but not so long as to feel like time had been wasted if the relationship didn't work out. "Cullen said you're a member of OMSAR. Does Christian belong, too?"

"No. He climbs and thought about joining, but he thinks I need something of my own, since we work together."

"Smart guy."

A dreamy expression filled Leanne's face. "Very smart and smokin' hot. Ever since we got together, I feel like I won the lottery."

"I know that feeling."

"With Doc?"

Cullen had treated Sarah with such respect from the moment they met. No other man in her life had ever done that. The cascade of memories made breathing difficult. She nodded.

"How did you meet?" Leanne asked.

"At the Red Rocks Rendezvous. We both lived in Seattle, and a mutual climbing acquaintance introduced us. A few hours later, we ended up in the same self-rescue clinic."

"Sounds like fate."

"Only if fate has a bad sense of humor."

Leanne's brow wrinkled. "Doc mentioned you're getting a divorce."

Sarah ignored the pang in her heart. "Yes."

"I've gotten to know him well over the past few months," Leanne admitted. "I had no clue he was married."

Sarah slumped into the couch. "He said he hadn't told people."

Leanne gave her a sympathetic nod. "If it's any consolation, I never saw Cullen flirt, let alone go out with another woman, if you were worried about that."

"Thanks." Hearing that was a relief, and what he'd told Sarah. "We've been separated for a year so if he'd wanted to…"

"Have you dated other guys?"

"No." She answered without any hesitation.

"Didn't think so." Leanne studied her. "When Doc moved here, he took himself way too seriously and had a stick up his butt. But he ended up being a good guy."

"He is." Just because they hadn't worked out didn't mean Sarah hated him. Part of her wished she could. "Not many men would bring their future ex-wives home to care for them."

"This is none of my business, but I'm still going to ask." Warmth and concern sounded in Leanne's voice. "Is there a possibility you'll reconcile?"

Sarah's heart thudded. Her biggest fear was allowing him to get close to her again. Yet a part of her didn't want to let him go, but she had to be realistic. A year had passed. He'd made no attempt to fight for her or even to talk about working things out. "No chance. We eloped in Las Vegas two days after we met. It was impulsive and romantic. The first few months were like living in paradise. But we shouldn't have jumped into marriage without getting to know each other better."

Oh, no. She touched her mouth. She'd said way too much.

Compassion filled Leanne's expression. "Love knows no logic."

Neither does lust. Sarah kept telling herself that was

what she'd felt for Cullen—not love. She'd been too afraid to let him fully inside her heart, afraid he would leave her like everyone else in her life had. But what they'd shared had been nice—at times, wonderful. She only wished the good parts could have lasted a little while longer.

Like forever.

Chapter Ten

The next morning, Cullen unlocked the cabin's front door. He yawned wide enough for a hummingbird to fit inside his mouth. The string of restless nights had caught up with him. He had one thought on his brain—sleep. He'd considered pulling off the road and taking a catnap, but he didn't want to keep Leanne any longer. He also wanted to see how Sarah was doing. He'd pulled out his cell phone more than once during his shift, but he hadn't wanted to wake them.

As he stepped into the cabin, the scent of freshly brewed coffee and something baking made his mouth water. He wasn't used to coming home to such a fragrant aroma. Caffeine would mess with his sleep, but his stomach growled for whatever was cooking.

Feminine laughter filled the air—something Cullen missed hearing. Sarah's laugh seeped into him, filling up the empty places inside with soothing warmth. He might have found a great place to live in a wonderful town with a supportive community, but something was missing from his life—a woman.

After the divorce, things will be better.

His mantra didn't make him feel as good as it had a couple of weeks ago.

In the living room, Sarah and Leanne sat on the couch.

"Good morning, ladies," he said.

"Hey, Doc." Leanne greeted him with a mock salute. "Just in time. The muffins will be ready in a few minutes."

Sarah stared at him. No excitement on her face. Nothing.

He would have appreciated some reaction from her. Maybe she was tired. Or hurting. He hoped not the latter.

"Busy shift?" Sarah asked.

Cardiac arrests, fractures, appendicitis, a gunshot victim, and two car accidents. Not to mention earaches, asthma attacks, fevers, and cuts. "Typical."

"That'll change next week," Leanne joked. "Full moon."

"Thanks for the warning." He noticed the two were paging through a magazine. "How did things go?"

"Fine," Sarah said. "I went to bed a half hour after Leanne arrived and woke up an hour ago."

"Easiest gig I've ever had. Sarah is the perfect patient." Leanne held up a thick bridal magazine full of glossy photographs. "She also has great wedding-planning advice."

"Wedding planning, huh?" That surprised Cullen. "I

suppose Sarah knows all about being married by an Elvis impersonator."

Leanne's mouth formed a perfect O. "You didn't tell me that, Sarah."

She shrugged. "I figured getting married in Vegas implied an Elvis impersonator."

"He had that jiggling-leg thing going on." Cullen demonstrated. "'Darlin', do you take this man…'"

Leanne laughed. "Where is my cell phone? No one will believe this. You *sound* like Elvis."

Sarah nodded. "We bought a wedding package that included a video of the ceremony. Each time I watch it, I'm amazed how well Cullen has nailed the voice."

His heart kicked in his chest. "You still watch the video?"

Sarah focused on the magazine. "I used to. It's packed away in a box somewhere."

Cullen hadn't expected she'd kept the video. He was sure she'd destroyed all evidence of their wedding. He wouldn't have been surprised if she'd gone so far as to toss her wedding ring into the garbage. He'd thought about getting rid of his and the framed photo she'd given him for their first anniversary but hadn't. He would toss both after the divorce was finalized.

The oven timer buzzed.

Leanne stood, went into the kitchen, and removed a muffin tin from the oven. "I hope you like blueberry."

A tight smile formed on Sarah's lips. "I love them. So does Cullen."

He remembered lazy mornings when he wasn't working. Sleeping in, taking a long shower, going to the corner coffee shop to pick up coffee and muffins.

Leanne put the muffins on a dinner plate and then carried them to the living room with salad plates, napkins, a knife, and butter.

"If you don't mind, I'm going to take off." She placed everything on the coffee table. "Christian is finished with his shift. This is the only day off we have together since the chief put us on different squads."

"Go have fun," Sarah said. "Thanks for staying with me, making muffins, and bringing me pants."

"Happy to help out. I'll see you when it's my turn again." Leanne grabbed her tote bag. "Be sure to go through the magazine and see what else you can come up with."

"Will do," Sarah said.

"I'll text you the link to my wedding boards on Pinterest. I'd love your input. I still can't decide on the favors."

Excitement lit up Sarah's face. Something that had been missing since he first saw her in the hospital. "I'd love to help."

Cullen eyed Sarah warily. Since when did she know anything about weddings?

"I'll see you out," Cullen said.

Leanne fell in step next to him. "Ever the gentleman."

He opened the door and followed her outside.

"I wondered why you didn't date," Leanne said.

"I figured it would be better to wait until the divorce was official."

"When will that be?"

"My attorney knows Sarah is staying with me. He thinks everything can be settled shortly."

"Sarah's great." Leanne raised her eyebrows. "You're sure a divorce is what you want?"

He hesitated. The automatic response hadn't come to him as quickly this time. "Sarah wants one, too, so don't get any ideas about playing matchmaker. Half the town has tried setting me up on blind dates. I don't need them interfering in my estranged marriage."

Leanne held up her hands. "Just asking. And since Sarah's staying with you, you're not as estranged as you were."

"Thomas."

A knowing grin lit up her face. "What?"

Cullen let it go. He knew she was only trying to help. "Thanks for staying with Sarah."

"You're welcome," Leanne said. "See you soon."

He went inside to find Sarah paging through the bridal magazine. Her muffins remained untouched. "Aren't you going to eat?"

She closed the magazine. "I was waiting for you."

That was polite. He sat next to her. "Do you want me to butter yours?"

"Thanks, but I've got it." Sarah placed a muffin on a plate. She awkwardly sliced the top and then added a pat of butter. "These smell so good."

Cullen took one. "Leanne's got a thing for muffins and chocolate."

Sarah rested her plate on the couch arm. "She's nice. I like her."

"I thought you might." He waited for Sarah to eat, but she didn't. Maybe she wasn't feeling well. "Leanne reminds me of you."

"I'm nothing like her."

"You both work in male-dominated environments. You're competent and intelligent. You ski and climb."

"Okay, I see the commonality." Sarah bit into the muffin. Finally. "But I wish I cooked as well as she does."

"Yeah, that would be nice."

She frowned. "I'm not that bad."

"I'm joking. You're a good cook." He motioned to the bridal magazine on her lap. "I'm curious how you know so much about wedding planning when we eloped."

She wiped her mouth with a napkin. "I told you I was engaged."

"I assumed it was a short engagement."

"Two and a half years."

Surprised, he drew back. "That's a long time."

"Longer when you add in the years we dated in high school."

He'd had no idea. "When was this?"

"Four years before I met you."

He did a quick calculation. "You must have been

young when you met him."

"Too young. And stupid," she admitted. "But I thought I knew better."

"Why didn't you tell me?" he asked.

"We got married two days after we met. I figured it didn't matter."

"That's a big part of your past."

Sarah shrugged.

Her not wanting to talk surprised him. Usually she wanted to pry every bit of information she could out of him. He set his half-eaten muffin on his plate. "What happened?"

She stared at the magazine. "Dylan entered my life at a time I felt very alone. I thought I was so lucky he wanted to be with me. There were some red flags, but after he proposed, I charged ahead with wedding plans. That morning…"

Cullen leaned toward her, feeling as if a cornice of snow had collapsed on top of him. "The morning of your wedding day?"

She nodded. "I was in a small room at the church. I was in college but also worked two jobs to buy my wedding gown and pay for the reception. I was fixing my veil when Dylan entered. He said he'd been up all night thinking about us, and had come to a conclusion. He couldn't marry me. The wedding was off."

Anger surged at how badly Sarah must have been hurt. Cullen balled his hands. "What a loser."

She shrugged. "He claimed I wasn't anything special.

That I would have kept him from having the future he wanted. I didn't blame him for not wanting to marry me."

"Don't say that." The words shot out of Cullen's mouth. "The guy had some serious issues if he thought any of those things about you."

"Yeah, issues with me." If Sarah was trying to sound lighthearted, she hadn't succeeded, which bothered Cullen more. "But I got over him. Moved on. Met you."

The conversation they'd had outside the wedding chapel in Las Vegas replayed.

Why don't we go inside and make things official? If we elope, you won't forget about me when we get back to Seattle or leave me standing at the altar after we've dated for years and I've planned a spectacular wedding for us.

Cullen remembered his reply.

I would never leave you like that.

Guilt lodged in his throat. He *had* left her. The minute she'd mentioned divorce, he'd hightailed it out of the apartment. His only thoughts had been on how hurt and betrayed he'd felt. Never once had he thought of her feelings.

Had mentioning divorce been a test? To see how committed he was?

Part of him wanted to be angry if she'd been testing him without his knowledge, yet…even if she hadn't been doing that, he'd failed. He'd run the second he had a chance. No wonder she'd freaked out on him whenever he tried to contact her about the divorce. "I'm sorry."

"No apologies needed. Getting jilted happened way

before you."

"I know, but I left you, too. If I'd known…"

"Would it have changed anything?"

Things hadn't been going well between them. She'd been pulling away from him. He'd hated how out of control he felt around her. "Probably not."

Sarah's lip quivered. "I appreciate your honesty."

"I appreciate you telling me about this."

A marble statue had a warmer expression than hers. "Better late than never."

Except it was too late to do anything about it now.

Or was it?

Would it have changed anything?

Probably not.

Cullen had reaffirmed Sarah's actions of a year ago. He'd even apologized. Something she'd never expected him to do. She should feel relieved she'd been spot-on about their relationship. Marriage had never tied them to each other as a couple, as husband and wife. Instead of relief, however, a heavy sadness bore down on her. Tilting her head to keep her tears at bay, she leaned against the couch.

"Need a refill?" Cullen asked from the kitchen.

"No, thanks." She flexed her fingers to stop her hand from shaking. "My cup is full."

She was used to the heartache and resentment over her failed marriage, so she wasn't sure why what Cullen had said bothered her so much.

Face it. Some people weren't cut out for marriage. Like her. Her parents. Must be in the DNA.

She glanced at the cover of the bridal magazine. The beautiful model dressed in a couture gown with perfectly applied makeup and coiffed hair glowed with a radiance Sarah envied. The woman wasn't a bride, but more thought had gone into the carefully executed photo shoot than into their eloping.

Yes, she'd put herself through school, earned a PhD even, but that didn't stop her from feeling that no matter what she did or how hard she tried, she was inadequate and destined to be alone. Her appetite disappeared.

Cullen returned with a steaming cup of coffee. "You seem better today."

"I'm getting there." Physically at least. Emotionally was another story. She rubbed her thumb against her fingertips. "You must be tired after work. Go to bed. I'll be fine while you sleep."

He raised his cup. "I got my second wind."

Maybe she should take a nap to give them a break from each other. She nearly laughed. Running off was Cullen's typical avoidance tactic, not hers.

"What's so funny?" he asked.

He'd been honest before. It was her turn. "I'm surprised you're still here."

He sipped his coffee. "Where would I go?"

"Anywhere I'm not."

"That's—"

"What you used to do," she interrupted. "You would disappear to the hospital, some mountain rescue thing, or wherever else you could go without me."

He tugged at his shirt collar. "I only did what I needed to do."

"Exactly."

She had never entered into the equation. It was almost as if he were different people. The doctor. The mountain rescuer. The lover. He hadn't embraced the role of husband. If anything, he'd worked hard not to.

"I don't want to argue," he said.

"We're not arguing," she countered. "We're having a discussion."

He took another sip. "Let's take a short walk outside."

She drummed her fingers on the sofa arm. "You're doing it again."

"Doing what?"

"Running away."

"I invited you."

Sarah shook her head. "You're trying to change the subject because you don't want to talk."

"All you want to do is talk, even when there's nothing to discuss."

Ouch. That stung. "I'll shut up, then."

"That's not..." He dragged his hand through his hair. "I don't want us to fight."

"This isn't anywhere close to fighting," she explained. "Sometimes when my parents fought, the police got involved. One of my stepfathers burned our clothes in the front yard. And my ex-fiancé…"

His jaw tightened. "Did he hurt you?"

"Not physically. But Dylan's words could be as powerful as a fist."

Cullen reached for her.

She moved away from him. His compassion and tenderness weren't what she needed. "I'm not proud I allowed the verbal abuse to happen for as long as it did or wasn't the one to break it off, but I knew where I stood with him."

"You know how I feel…*felt* about you."

Seriously? She couldn't believe he said that. "At first, yes, but later…."

"There's no reason to bring this up now." He stood. "I'm going for a walk. If you'd rather stay inside…"

"No." The word spewed from her mouth like lava out of Mount Etna. "I want to go outside."

A beat passed. And another. "Come on then."

Five minutes later, she stood on Cullen's driveway in her boots. She couldn't fit her cast in the sleeve of her jacket, so she wore the right side over her shoulder. The sharp scent of pine wafted on the breeze. She inhaled, filling her lungs with the crisp mountain air.

"Isn't this better than arguing inside?" Cullen asked.

"It's nice, but the inside wasn't so bad." Sunlight kissed her cheeks. She'd missed feeling the warmth on her face. "The best part of disagreeing is making up."

"I don't think so."

"That's because you never stuck around for the make-up sex."

Cullen started to speak but then pressed his lips together.

Maybe that hadn't been nice of her to say, but she couldn't help herself.

Humming a little tune, Sarah moved away from him. For the first time in a long while, she had the upper hand. She wanted to savor the moment.

Leaves and twigs crunched under her feet. She strolled along the edge of the road.

He caught up to her. "Is there a statute of limitation on make-up sex?"

Sarah froze. "Why do you want to know?"

Wicked laughter lit his eyes. "Seems I missed out."

She raised her chin. "Your loss."

His charming smile unleashed a colony of bats in her stomach. "Yours, too."

Her muscles tensed. She hadn't expected him to respond this way. That was her mistake, because this was what he'd always done when she would get upset. Turn off the serious side. Get all sexy and fun and flirty. Make her insides hot and gooey. He hadn't changed one bit.

But Sarah had.

As her heart pounded like a jackhammer, she casually lifted one shoulder. "You win some. You lose some."

He stepped closer. Too close for anything other than

kissing her.

He wouldn't, would he? She gulped, not sure what she wanted the answer to be. Okay, she knew. But *yes* wasn't the correct response if she wanted to play it safe.

He cocked a brow. "So the statute…"

Temptation flared, only to be tempered by common sense. What she wanted warred with what she needed, but self-preservation reigned supreme.

Her fingernails dug into her palms. "Expired."

Sarah marched down the road as if her life depended on putting distance between them. Her abdomen ached, but she kept going. She didn't know where, nor did she care.

Cullen grabbed her hand. "Slow down. You'll hurt yourself."

"I'm fine."

"No, you're not. You're mad at me. Even madder than you were inside."

She pressed her lips together, not about to give him the satisfaction of being correct.

"Don't deny it." He pointed to her forehead. "I know because you have a crease between your eyebrows."

Sarah touched the spot.

He moved her finger. "Right here."

She felt the line but still wasn't going to admit he had figured that out about her.

Cullen glanced to his right. "Look."

"What?"

"Shh." Cullen touched her lips with his finger before moving behind her. His chest pressed against her back. Bringing his arm around her, he pointed. "A doe and two fawns."

Awareness hummed through Sarah. He emanated heat and strength. Her pulse raced.

She couldn't focus. Bigfoot could have been standing in front of her, and she wouldn't have noticed him.

Her reaction made zero sense given her anger, resentment, and hurt over their breakup. Their marriage was over. Yet, her body didn't seem to understand that.

"See them?" he whispered.

The warmth of his breath against her neck sent chills racing through her. Her gaze followed the length of his arm until she saw the deer. A momma and her two babies, munching on a bush.

Her breath stilled. "So cute."

"I've seen these three around the cabin before," he said quietly.

The deer ate without glancing at them. The fawns were more interested in keeping an eye on their mother, who paid close attention to them.

Sarah wished her mom had cared as much for her. Wished Cullen had, too.

She shoved her free hand into her jacket pocket. "I haven't noticed them or any others."

"You haven't been here long, but you will."

It felt as if she'd been here forever. And not in a good way. "I'll be on the lookout."

The doe stiffened. She stared in their direction and then past them, as if she sensed something.

The sound of an engine splintered the silence.

As a car passed, the deer bounded into the trees, her two fawns following.

If only Sarah could do the same. Not head into the forest, but go home to Bellingham. She wanted to pretend none of this had happened—her accident and her injuries and her reaction to Cullen. She wanted the confusing emotions to go away.

He faced her. "They'll be back."

What she and Cullen had once shared was gone. A longing for what would never be filled her heart. A sigh welled inside her. She parted her lips.

He lowered his head and kissed her.

Sarah's heart stalled.

His kiss was gentle and sweet. He only touched her with his lips. But that was enough.

Nerve endings stirred to life as if awakened from a deep slumber. Pleasurable sensations pulsed through her. She'd forgotten how wonderful he kissed.

He moved away from her.

Sarah took a step back. Swallowed. "Why did you do that?"

"Make-up kiss."

A nervous laugh spilled out. She didn't know what else to do...say.

"The statute of limitations for a make-up kiss has to be longer than for make-up sex," he added.

"If it isn't, I won't press charges."

He grinned wryly. "That's generous of you, Lavagirl."

Her lips tingled. "Only repaying your generosity, Dr. Gray."

His smile spread, matching the heat flowing through her.

If she wasn't careful, he could overwhelm her. The way he had in Las Vegas. That wouldn't be good or safe. "But we shouldn't make kisses a habit."

"You're probably right about that," Cullen agreed. "As long as we don't argue, we should be fine."

Probably. Should be. He'd left wiggle room.

On purpose? She couldn't say.

That meant Sarah had to make sure nothing more happened, because even though she knew better, she couldn't deny wanting more kisses.

Chapter Eleven

In the house, Cullen unloaded the dishwasher. He couldn't believe he'd kissed Sarah.

A momentary lapse? If that had been the case, he would have kissed her with more passion. He'd been careful to keep things under control due to her injuries and emotional state. Not easy with the images of make-up sex shuffling through his mind. But he had enjoyed the kiss.

The talk leading up to it... Not so much.

Had he run away as she said?

Cullen had escaped a few times whenever his control slipped or he was too overwhelmed by her. But she had to be exaggerating the number, caught up in some revised history of their marriage to make her feel less guilty for bringing up a divorce.

With the kitchen clean, he peeked into her room.

She was sound asleep.

Good. Cullen needed to rest himself. He was running

on caffeine. But he wanted to do something first. He entered his room, closed the door, and made a call on his cell phone.

"Hey, Doc," Sean Hughes, one of the OMSAR rescue team leaders, answered. "How's Sarah?"

"Napping. She's doing better."

"Good to hear."

Cullen adjusted the phone at his ear. "I'm signed up for your ready team tomorrow, but I want to stay home with Sarah."

"No worries," Sean said. "We'll get the spot covered."

"Thanks, and I'm sorry."

"No apology necessary." He didn't sound upset. "Family first. Do what you have to do."

Cullen was trying to do that. Even though he wasn't sure why.

A week later, sunlight streamed through Sarah's bedroom window. Not that good weather would change her agenda for the day. Physical therapy and a walk were the highlights. She'd had a follow-up visit with a physician about her sutures, which meant being stuck at the cabin until her visit to the orthopedist next week.

At least she could look forward to getting out of the house for that.

Yeah, doctor visits were the most fun she had these days.

Forcing herself out of bed, she combed her fingers through her hair. Maybe she could work on her laptop for a few minutes. She couldn't manage much longer than that. Headaches and her arm limited productivity.

As she headed toward the kitchen, the scent of freshly brewed coffee and something baking filled the air. Sarah's mouth watered at the tantalizing aromas. Her tummy grumbled.

The delicious smells wafting in the house told her Zoe Hughes, who was scheduled to be Sarah's babysitter, wasn't here. The former socialite, married to Sean, was beautiful and friendly, but she couldn't cook. Hannah had been here yesterday, so that meant Carly or Leanne.

Unless it was…Cullen.

The thought gave Sarah an unexpected boost of energy. She quickened her pace.

She hadn't seen him in days. He'd been working his shifts and covering for other doctors. He'd explained he was doing this due to the time he'd spent in Seattle with her, not to get away from the house—she assumed he meant her. He'd even called to say hello, something he'd never done, which Sarah appreciated.

But his absences reminded her of how she'd been so desperate to see him when they lived together. She wasn't desperate now. More…eager. The logic behind her eagerness couldn't be readily explained, but her frustration could be.

Sarah's slow recovery gave her insight into how magma must feel rising out of the earth's mantle and into the crust. She wasn't a mix of solids, melt, and gases, but the physics behind recovering from her injuries was similar and taking too much time.

In the hallway, Sarah noticed someone in the kitchen. Someone with brown hair. Someone female with two braids.

Not Cullen.

Leanne.

Sarah stumbled but regained her balance before she fell. She'd experienced a lifetime of disappointments, everything from forgotten birthdays to being jilted on her wedding day to having her marriage disintegrate. Not seeing Cullen this morning was nothing in the grand scheme of things.

Leanne greeted Sarah. "You're up early."

"I went to bed around eight." Sarah hadn't been that tired, but she'd wanted Hannah to go home and say goodnight to her three children. Being tucked in meant a lot to kids. Sarah wished her parents had done that with her.

Cullen must have come and gone while she was sleeping. If he'd returned home at all. A few times, he hadn't. Not knowing where he'd been bugged her.

Sarah leaned against the breakfast bar. "I thought Zoe was going to be here."

"She had to run to Portland, so two of us are tag-teaming it." Leanne picked up the coffeepot. "You're stuck with me until lunchtime."

"You're the one who's stuck." These women were so kind and friendly. "I appreciate what you're doing for me."

"It's our pleasure." The sincerity in Leanne's voice touched Sarah's heart. "This is what friends do for each other."

Cullen was so lucky. Hood Hamlet was a special place. A perfect place for a family.

As Leanne poured coffee into two cups, light glimmered off her diamond engagement ring. The paramedic had found her one true love at the fire station. A younger man who adored her, according to Zoe.

Sarah felt a pang. Maybe happy-ever-afters were possible for some people. She hoped so for her new friend's sake.

"Sit." Leanne placed the steaming mugs on the table. "I baked banana-nut muffins."

Sarah sat. "I like those as much as blueberry ones."

"I know." Leanne grinned. "Cullen told me all your favorites."

Sarah drew back. "He did?"

"I wanted to make sure I made things you liked."

Oh, Leanne must have asked. Still, that Cullen remembered was nice. "Thanks."

People in Hood Hamlet took care of each other and strangers like her, too. Home-cooked, healthy meals arrived each day. Though Cullen had been away so much he'd ended up with leftovers. When he came home…

Her throat tightened.

Cullen hadn't fallen into the same pattern of their marriage, but the longer he stayed away, the more she worried he might.

Leanne carried a platter of muffins to the table. "Dig in."

"Thanks." Sarah bit into one. The flavors and warmth filled her mouth. "Delicious. I like the walnuts."

"Me, too."

She took another bite but couldn't stop thinking about Cullen. That added to her growing frustrations over her injuries and inability to work much. She shoved a piece of the muffin into her mouth.

Concern clouded Leanne's brown eyes. "Taking it easy is difficult for you."

Sarah stared into her coffee cup. "Relaxing and resting is downright aggravating."

"Cullen says you're improving every day."

Hurt sliced through Sarah. He hadn't told her that. Okay, she shouldn't take his silence personally. She wasn't his friend or a climbing and ski partner like Leanne.

Sarah shook it off.

So what if he'd kissed her? Or spent two whole days and a night taking care of her before he'd returned to a marathon of shift coverages?

She was a temporary roommate and no longer a permanent part of his life—a life she was beginning to envy after a week and a half in Hood Hamlet.

Being envious of Leanne was silly.

Everything Sarah wanted and cared about was in Bellingham. Mount Baker. The institute. Her postdoc.

Leanne studied her. "Since you're doing better, you should get out of the cabin for more than a walk."

Anticipation made Sarah sit straighter. "I would love that."

"Zoe wants to go to Taco Night at the brewpub this evening. Join us."

Sarah's stomach fluttered. "Sounds like fun, but I don't know if Cullen will agree. He can't turn off the doctor switch."

Leanne grinned. "I'll talk to him. Convince him going out will be good for you."

"He still might say no."

"Then I'll ask Bill Paulson to help me kidnap you. He's been my best friend since I was nine. He's up for anything."

Sarah raised a brow. "Even kidnapping?"

"Pretty much," Leanne said. "He might draw the line at disposing of a body, but with Paulson you never know, especially if a beautiful woman is involved."

A smile tugged at the corners of Sarah's lips. "Sounds like an interesting guy."

Leanne sipped her coffee. "He's a real-life Peter Pan who will never grow up, but he's also a total sweetheart. You'll meet him after lunch. He's staying with you until Cullen gets home."

Sarah perked up. "Cullen will be home tonight?"

"This afternoon. That's why tonight is perfect for going out."

"I'd enjoy that." Especially if she could be with Cullen.

"It'll happen." Leanne sounded so confident.

"And if not, you and Paulson can kidnap me."

A fake kidnapping sounded fun. Other than the doctor's appointment and a couple of walks, Sarah had been lying around since she'd arrived. Now, if she'd been lying around with Cullen…

Heat rocketed through her. Uh-oh. Better stick to thinking about Taco Night. Mexican food was as spicy as she could handle.

In the hospital cafeteria, Cullen stared at the crumbs from the fish and chips on his plate. He sipped his coffee. The caffeine would get him through the next two hours.

A good thing he needed to cover only eight hours today. He'd spent the past five days covering shifts for others and working his own. He'd stayed at an anesthesiologist's house rather than drive home only to return a few hours later.

Cullen enjoyed this reprieve from Sarah. Being with her messed with his head. He didn't want her getting anywhere close to his heart.

These days away from her, however, intensified his

guilt. Not only for leaving Sarah the way he had a year ago, but also for running away from her when they'd been living together as husband and wife. She'd been right calling him out on what he'd done in Seattle. He had ignored the truth then, but he saw it now.

No wonder she'd been unhappy. After the way her jerk of an ex-fiancé had dumped her, Cullen's actions must have been hurtful and seemed like a betrayal, even if he'd only been trying to protect himself.

An excuse?

Maybe, but the depth of his attraction and obsession with Sarah had frightened him. He'd found himself totally wrapped up in her. Every second of every day, she would be on his mind unless he pushed her aside and kept himself distracted. For the first time, he'd understood his brother's need for another fix. Blaine had found his escape and relief in drugs, but Cullen had been doing the same with Sarah. She was his addiction, making him forget the past and his troubles. The delirious happiness she provided was intoxicating. To keep from losing himself completely as his brother had, he'd had to pull back.

But he'd never told her his reasons. Never told her about Blaine. Never shared the pain that had made Cullen the man he was today.

He didn't think he could.

But he never wanted to hurt her that way again. That was why he'd told her about making up shifts this week so she didn't think he had an ulterior motive for working so much.

And even though he wasn't with her, he thought about Sarah every day. More like several times each day. Wondered how her recovery was going. Wondered if she missed him as much as he missed her.

Unable to deny his curiosity any longer, he called Leanne. She'd texted him this morning saying she was with Sarah instead of Zoe.

"Hey," Leanne answered. "I was going to call you."

His shoulder muscles tensed. "Sarah okay?"

"She's great. Looking better than she has all week. Stronger, too."

Relief washed over him. "Good."

"Sarah is doing so well you should bring her to Taco Night."

He hadn't been to the brewpub in three weeks or seen his friends, other than those who'd dropped off food or were helping out, but tonight was too soon for Sarah. "She's not up for going out."

"She wants to go," Leanne said to his surprise. "She needs to get out of the cabin."

"Sarah isn't a social butterfly. She's a scientist who would rather be on a volcano than anywhere else."

"Come on, Doc." Leanne had probably rolled her eyes. "It's not some fancy soiree. It's tacos at Jake's brewpub."

Except for one thing. Everyone Cullen knew would be there. Questions would be asked. Some he wasn't sure he wanted to—or even could—answer. Yes, he was using

Sarah as an excuse, but so what? This was where *he* lived. He didn't want her becoming a part of his new life. "She'll get too tired."

"I don't know how she's managed staying in the cabin this long." Disapproval rang clear in Leanne's voice. "Just sitting around isn't good for her morale or her recovery."

But it was safe. For them both. "She does need to get out more, but next week will be better."

"Maybe for you, but not Sarah. You can stay home tonight. Paulson will bring her."

Cullen laughed. "You want Paulson to take my wife to Taco Night?"

"It's not a problem," Leanne said. "He's with Sarah right now. The two hit it off."

Cullen's heart went splat against the cafeteria floor.

"What?" His voice rose. He lowered it. "You texted you were with her."

"This morning. I had to attend a Christmas Magic in Hood Hamlet meeting after lunch. No worries. Paulson will take good care of Sarah."

Cullen was afraid of that. His collar tightened.

He trusted Sarah. But Paulson…not so much.

Chapter Twelve

Bill Paulson sat next to Sarah on the couch with an impish grin on his lips and a suggestive gleam in his gaze. "So what do you want to do now?"

Charming might describe Hood Hamlet, but the adjective didn't come close to describing the friendly, easy-on-the-eyes firefighter in well-worn jeans and a faded T-shirt. Sarah enjoyed spending time with him. He made her feel feminine and pretty even when she resembled a boxer, albeit one who'd been out of the ring for a couple of weeks.

"I have no idea," she admitted.

The guy could give any pop-star pretty boy a run for the money in the looks department *and* kick their butts with his athletic build, but his sense of humor appealed to her the most. Hanging out with him was fun despite his acting a tad immature with not-so-subtle, yet humorous innuendos.

"You've kept me entertained all afternoon. I'm not

sure what else we can do," she added.

"I'm sure I can think of a few things." Mischief sounded in his voice.

Bill Paulson would be considered a catch, except for two things—the guy knew he was attractive and he was an incorrigible flirt. No way would she encourage him.

He rubbed his chin. "I could paint your toenails. That has to be tough to do with your dominant hand in a cast."

Okay, the guy was a good listener. He'd taken their earlier discussion on being right-handed and come up with this. But however tempting that might sound, she could survive without nail polish. The only man who should be painting her toenails was Cullen. Not that he would. Or that she would ask him. "Thanks, but a nap would be better."

He scrambled off the couch. "I'll fluff your pillows. Be right back."

Sarah laughed at his eagerness to help. Bill was half player, half Boy Scout rolled into one. Adorable, but a handful for a single woman who happened to be attracted to him. Neither of which she was.

The front door opened. Leanne must be back.

Sarah went to say hello, but the word died on her lips.

Cullen stormed inside, wearing his scrubs. Lines bracketed his mouth.

"The bed's ready," Bill announced from the hallway.

Cullen's face reddened. A muscle pulsed in his jaw.

Bill grinned. "Hey, Doc. I've been taking good care of Sarah."

Cullen balled his fingers. He acted as if he wanted to punch someone. "I'll bet you have."

Sarah had never seen him act this way. She didn't like it. "Cullen?"

He glared at Bill. "What's this about a bed being ready?"

Bill held up his hands in front of him, as if to surrender. "Dude, I don't know what's got into you, but if you're thinking I'd put the moves on your pretty wife, you're way off. I just fluffed her pillows."

Cullen's intense gaze bounced from Bill to her. "You fluffed her what?"

"Her pillows," Bill said.

"The pillows on my bed," Sarah clarified. "I wanted to nap."

"A nap," Cullen repeated.

"A nap," Bill reaffirmed.

Cullen seemed to digest the information. She didn't know what his problem was. She smiled at Bill. "You've been a big help this afternoon."

"Anytime." Bill kissed her cheek, rather bravely she thought. "If you need a ride to Taco Night…"

"I'm taking her." Cullen's demanding tone left no room for argument. "After her nap."

Bill pulled out his car keys from his pocket. A grin twitched at his lips. "Looks like my work here is done."

"Thanks for the brownies," she said, still unsure

what was going on with Cullen when Bill had been nothing but helpful and sweet.

"You made her brownies?" Cullen asked incredulously.

"I made you both brownies. Well, my mom did." Bill had explained how his mom cooked his meals, cleaned his house, and did his laundry. No wonder the guy hadn't grown up yet. He didn't need to. "She dropped them off at my house this morning."

Sarah stood. "Thank your mom for us. And thanks for keeping me company."

"My pleasure." Bill glanced at Cullen. "Your wife is quite the card shark. She kicked my butt at Texas hold 'em. A good thing we weren't playing strip poker, or I'd have been buck naked in no time."

A murderous expression formed on Cullen's face.

Bill didn't seem to care. Or maybe he didn't notice. "See you at the brewpub, Sarah. If Doc changes his mind about going, give me a call."

With that, Bill left.

Cullen stood next to the breakfast bar. His lips narrowed. "Please tell me you know better than to get involved with a guy like Paulson."

Defensiveness rose. "Get involved? What are you talking about?"

"A lot of women like him."

Sarah didn't appreciate Cullen's tone. "Bill's a nice guy."

"He's a total player who will never grow up."

She saw that and didn't need Cullen pointing it out. "You're jealous."

"No, I'm not," he said with a dismissive air.

"Then why did you storm into the house like a bull from the streets of Pamplona wanting a fight?"

He took a deep breath and another, as if reining himself in yet again. "I was worried."

"Worried."

"I like Paulson," Cullen admitted. "But he'll hit on any woman."

"You thought he would hit on me."

He clenched his teeth. "You deserve better."

Sarah had deserved better from Cullen, too. She raised her chin. "Yes, I do. Bill is a big flirt, but it was innocent, all in fun."

"He didn't—"

"He was a perfect gentleman."

Cullen's brow furrowed. "*Gentleman* and *Paulson* don't belong in the same sentence."

"Maybe you don't know him as well as you think you do." This macho act of Cullen's didn't impress her. "Bill made me laugh and feel better than I've felt since long before the accident." Cullen opened his mouth to speak, but she continued. "But even if I swallowed a 'stupid' pill and threw caution to the wind, I would never get involved with Bill...with any man...because you and I are still married."

Relief washed over Cullen's face. "Good."

His response angered and confused her. Why would

he care, if he wanted a divorce? "That's all you have to say?"

"What more do you want?"

"An apology," she ordered. "You charged in here assuming the worst without considering that Bill is your friend and I'm your wife."

"I haven't been thinking straight. I've...been working a lot."

"What's new?" She didn't need to explain, but she didn't want him thinking the worst of her. "Just so you know, I have been good. Very good. Doing everything you and Dr. Marshall told me to do. Which is more than I can say for you."

Lines creased Cullen's forehead. "I have no idea what you're talking about."

"You told me you had shifts to make up, but you haven't been here at all. Heaven only knows where you've been spending your nights."

A devilish grin lit up his face. "You're the jealous one."

"Am not." Okay, maybe a little. But she didn't dare admit that to him. "I was...worried."

"Worried."

More than she wanted to admit. More than he would ever know. "Yes."

He grinned sheepishly. "The way I was worried about you and Bill."

Busted. She nodded once, feeling petty and pathetic.

His gaze met hers. "No need for you to worry. I

stayed at a friend's place near the hospital in order to sleep more between shifts."

"Makes sense to stay with a friend."

But she didn't know if his "friend" was male or a buxom blonde. And Sarah wanted to know. Badly.

Cullen strode toward the couch. "I'm learning how important it is to have friends at work and outside the job. I realize I've been taking them for granted."

The way he'd taken her for granted. But he'd never considered her a friend. They'd gone from "hello" to "I do" in two days.

Sarah's throat tightened.

She should say something, but she hadn't a clue what. Something from an earlier conversation popped into her head. "You shouldn't get a pet if you're gone so much."

His eyes widened. "I don't always work this many shifts. A cat might work. As you said, they're independent."

"Even cats need to feel wanted and loved."

Not that he wanted and loved her, but he once had. At least, that was what he'd told her. His actions at first suggested he'd meant the words.

Cullen stood next to her.

Sarah's pulse kicked up. Tension simmered between them. She shouldn't want him to kiss her. But she did. Badly.

Look away. Move away.

But she couldn't—okay, she didn't want to. His full

lips mesmerized her.

Once again, the situation reminded her of magma rising. Only this time moving closer to the surface, where the gas pressure increased, accelerating faster and faster until erupting.

She wet her lips.

Cullen remained focused on her. "In case you're still worried, the friend I stayed with—he's an anesthesiologist from the hospital."

The surge of relief did nothing to douse the flame building inside her, threatening to explode. "Thanks."

The blue of his eyes deepened. "Thank you."

"For what?"

"This." Cullen lowered his mouth to hers and kissed her.

Heaven. His kiss made Sarah feel like she had died and gone to heaven. Best to enjoy every second, every minute, if she was that lucky. This might be as close as she ever got to the pearly gates while her heart still beat. And beating it was.

In triple time.

His lips moved over hers with skill and familiarity. The kiss brought her home, to where she'd longed to be for months…in his arms. She'd thought about him, dreamed about him, missed him, even though she should have been getting over him. But now she understood why moving on was so difficult.

He tasted warm and inviting.

This was a yummy, comfy place she never wanted to

leave. Each touch of his mouth, of his hands, made her tingle inside.

Forget pain medication—his kisses were all she needed to feel better. Her blood simmered, rushing through her veins. She hadn't felt wanted in so long she didn't want the feeling to end.

His hand ran up her back, caressing her, until his fingers were in her hair.

More. She wanted more.

Sarah parted her lips. He accepted the invitation and deepened the kiss, pressing harder against her mouth. She remembered the times they'd kissed before. Remembered the good in their marriage when she had believed they'd be together forever. Maybe the concussion caused her memories to be hazy, but this kiss felt different. Better, somehow.

She didn't want to analyze it. She wanted to…enjoy.

Heat pooled deep inside her. Need ached. Grew.

A moan escaped her lips.

More. Please.

Cullen drew her closer. She arched into him, only to come to an abrupt stop. She crashed into something, sending a jagged pain through her sore and healing abdomen. Her lips slipped off his.

Air rushed out of her lungs. Spots appeared. Pain weakened her knees. She hurt so badly, but Cullen held on to her so she didn't fall.

He groaned but didn't let go.

Sarah forced herself to breathe. A knife sliced

through her midsection.

As she straightened, the pain intensified.

Stupid cast.

With the permanent bend in her elbow, her arm was stuck in position at least until her appointment with the orthopedist next week, a barrier between her and Cullen.

A weapon.

Despite hurting, she couldn't deny her reaction to Cullen's kisses. Her swollen and bruised lips throbbed. Her heart beat wildly. Her pulse hadn't settled.

She wanted to rewind time and relive each second.

That was...dumb.

Forget about the cast getting in the way—she should have known better than to kiss him the way she had. "I'm so sorry."

Cullen bent over, gasping for air. He lowered his arms from around her, and she nearly toppled over. "Give me a sec."

The rasp in his voice told Sarah he was hurting, too.

She glanced at her cast. "Dangerous."

He stared at the floor. "You have no idea."

Oh, but Sarah did. She needed to sit but didn't trust her legs to hold out. Standing was difficult enough. She leaned against the couch and took a breath.

Still doubled over, Cullen glanced her way. His gaze sharpened. He straightened. "You're hurt."

Not trusting her voice, she nodded.

"Let me see if you're bleeding." He raised her shirt. Relief shone on his face. "You're not."

"You okay?"

He straightened. "I can breathe now. How about you?"

Her senses reeled. Her heart screamed for more kisses. Her incisions hurt. "I've been better. But the pain's subsiding quicker than it usually does."

Cullen's mouth twisted, making his expression more serious. As if the fate of the world rested on his shoulders and he'd screwed things up. "This was…"

"A mistake." Better for her to admit the truth before him. "If you're worried I think this changes things between us, don't be. The other kiss didn't. This one won't, either."

He didn't speak, but his dark gaze remained on her.

"Kisses are an old habit for us. It was bound to happen. The opportunity arose again. I wanted to be kissed." Rambling, she tried to justify what happened and her actions. "We'll look back at this and laugh someday."

He raised a brow. "You think?"

She had no idea, but laughing this off was better than analyzing their every interaction to death and not liking the conclusion. "Sure."

"Most kisses aim for romance, not humor."

Had he been aiming for romance by kissing her?

Her pulse accelerated. No more kisses. "True, but romantic kisses are a dime a dozen. This one…"

A grin tugged at his lips. He rubbed his stomach. "I won't be forgetting this one any time soon."

Her, either, but for different reasons than his.

Warning bells sounded in her head.

Who was she kidding? She was past the warning stage. Alarms blared.

Best not to travel this road again. Giving in to desire would lead to more heartache. "It won't happen again."

"Definitely not."

That was fast. Almost too fast.

He'd said *probably* before but used *definitely* this time.

Disappointment spiraled to the tips of her toes. At least they agreed, right?

She pressed her lips together, unsure what to say or do next. That seemed to be standard operating procedure around Cullen. So why had she been so eager to see him when she woke this morning?

He went into the kitchen. "You mentioned taking a nap. While you sleep, I'll figure out dinner. I'm sure we have enough leftovers."

"It's Taco Night at the brewpub."

"You're in pain."

She didn't want to stay in the cabin with him. "I want to go out."

He assessed her as if she were one of his patients. "The brewpub will be too much for you after such a long day."

"I've done nothing but lie or sit around, except for a walk outside with Bill."

Cullen's jaw clenched. "There's snow on the ground. You could have slipped."

"We didn't go far, and Bill never let go of my arm."

"How gentlemanly of him."

Sarah didn't appreciate Cullen's sarcastic tone, but maybe she could use this to her advantage. "Do you want to go to the brewpub tonight or not?"

"I enjoy Taco Night, but I'm happy to stay home. It's been a long week."

She empathized with that. "You must be exhausted."

He opened the refrigerator. "Let's go next week."

"You can go then." She straightened. "I'm going tonight. I'll call Bill."

Cullen slammed the fridge door. "Why do you want to go so badly?"

"I'm desperate to get out of the house."

He arched a brow. "Desperate?"

Sarah nodded. "I've been doing everything I'm supposed to do, but enough is enough. I need to get out and do something other than see a doctor. Have…"

"Fun," he finished for her.

Kissing him again would be fun. She couldn't admit that to him, not after calling the recent one a mistake. "Lying around resting is the antithesis of fun. I can sit at the brewpub as easily as I can here."

"You won't be alone."

That was the problem. If she stayed at the cabin, she would be alone with him. "I enjoy having people around while you're at work. Everyone is nice, and we're getting to know each other. But I need to get out, have a change of environment, scenery, whatever you want to call it, or I'm going to lose my mind."

Or burn with unspent desire.

Kissing Cullen again would send her over the edge completely.

Going to the brewpub made the most sense. The other option—spending the evening at home with Cullen—wasn't a smart idea. Sure, they'd agreed not to kiss again, but they'd also agreed to divorce. Who knew what could happen if they stayed here alone tonight? She didn't want to take any chances. She couldn't afford more kisses. Losing her heart to him again would destroy her.

"Leanne mentioned the soft pretzels with the house dipping sauce," Sarah explained. "I'll be able to have tacos and pretzels. Two things I love."

"I didn't know you like pretzels."

She wished they could have gotten to know each other better outside the bedroom.

"I didn't know about your broken arm." Sarah waited for him to respond. She didn't understand his hesitation. "If you'd rather stay home, that's fine. Bill will drive me if you're not up for it."

Cullen's nostrils flared. "I'm up for it."

"But you said—"

"I changed my mind, okay?"

More than okay. She didn't care if jealousy was the reason or not, but an unexpected rush of feminine power flowed through her. "It's great. Thanks."

"Take a nap first," he ordered in that oh-so-strict doctor's voice of his.

She gave a mock salute. "Aye, aye, Captain. Pillows

161

are fluffed, and the sheet turned down, sir."

If only he'd join her…

Playful images flitted through her mind.

On second thought, napping by herself was better. Safer. Even if she would be…lonelier.

Chapter Thirteen

Taco Night at the Hood Hamlet Brewpub usually made Cullen happy. Nothing beat good food, great beer, and hanging with friends, but this was the last place he wanted to be tonight. With his fingers white-knuckled around the steering wheel, he drove onto Main Street, trying to ignore the floral scent of Sarah drifting his way.

He focused his attention on the road. She was the one with the concussion, but he needed to have his head examined. Imagining her with Paulson during the drive home had done crazy things to Cullen.

His self-control had been nonexistent. Whenever Sarah was involved, his feelings overrode common sense. But he hadn't withdrawn or run away from her. This time, he'd done something worse. He'd kissed her.

Talk about reckless behavior.

Finding out *she* was jealous about who he was with had been a real turn-on. Kissing her had seemed the most natural thing in the world. But he couldn't allow himself to be captivated by her again.

Her kisses had sent him to the brink. He'd been on the verge of losing control until she'd taken him out with her cast. He'd never been so relieved to be punched in the gut.

The pain was going away, but he could have hurt himself more if the kissing continued.

And Sarah.

She was still healing, yet he hadn't handled her with care. Kissing her had made him forget her injuries. They were lucky the consequences hadn't been worse.

She peered out the window. "It's crowded for a weeknight."

"Fresh snowfall brings spring skiers and riders to the mountain."

Sarah angled toward him. "What about climbers?"

"If climbers are smart, they'll wait for a better weather window and an avalanche report."

"If not?"

He parked across the street from the brewpub. "You hope they get lucky. Otherwise, OMSAR pings us with a mission callout."

"Some people think they can conquer the mountain."

He turned off the engine. "Yeah, but the mountain always wins."

"Mother Nature gets a shot once in a while."

The way she touched her stomach made him wonder if she was still in pain. Going out was not a good idea.

"Leanne's fiancé can tell you all about that."

"She mentioned how OMSAR rescued his cousin and him."

Cullen pulled the key out of the ignition. "They got caught in a wicked storm, but it ended well."

Sarah unfastened her seat belt. "It's too bad there aren't more happy endings like that."

Her wistful tone surprised him. Sarah didn't give in to flights of fancy or fairy tales. She must be talking about her rescue. "Yours has a happy ending."

"What are you talking about?"

"Mount Baker. Your accident," he explained. "Your data could have been destroyed. Your injuries could have been worse. You could have died. But none of those things happened. Happy ending."

"It will be happy once I'm back at the institute."

Away from him.

The words, unspoken but implied, stung given how passionately she'd kissed him earlier this afternoon.

She fumbled with the door handle.

He leaned over to help. His arm brushed her chest, sending a burst of heat rushing through him. He pulled back. "Sorry."

"I've got it." On the third try, she opened the door.

She exited as if a bomb were about to blow. He hurried around the truck. When he held out his hand, she took it. "Be careful."

Annoyance burned in the depths of Sarah's eyes. She tugged away from him. "I know to be careful."

"Just watching out for you."

"It's not as if I made the wrong decision or did something stupid to make myself fall." She spoke in a rush. "I was doing my job. If the steam blast hadn't happened…"

She wouldn't be here. The thought brought a strange mix of relief and regret.

"I can cross the street by myself," she continued.

"There could be ice." Sarah must be hungry. Hunger would explain her short fuse. "I'd say the same thing to anyone else who was with me, so don't get your panties in a twist."

"That would be impossible to do, since I'm not wearing panties."

Cullen's mouth went dry. His gaze dropped to her legging-covered hips.

"Trust me, I'd know if my thong was twisted," she added.

A thong. He remembered her thongs.

His temperature spiraled. He needed to take off his jacket.

Uh-oh. She was crossing the street without him. "Wait up, Lavagirl."

Sarah stood on the sidewalk, tapping her toe.

"You're hungry," he said.

Her foot stopped moving. She nodded with a contrite expression.

"The taco bar is all you can eat," he said.

She bit her lip.

"But you can order those pretzels first." He motioned her toward the entrance, but she didn't move.

Uncertainty flashed on her face. "Is there anything I should know before we go inside?"

"About the taco bar?"

"About the people I'm going to meet."

Not only hungry. Nervous. "You've met Zoe, Hannah, and Leanne."

"And Bill."

Unfortunately. Cullen wasn't too happy with Paulson right now. "Jake Porter who owns the place, Sean Hughes, and Christian Welton, if he's not on duty, will be here. I'm not sure about Hannah and Garrett Willingham, Rita and Tim Moreno, or Carly, since they have kids and need babysitters. You never know who will show up. But no worries. Everybody is nice."

An older couple holding hands exited the brewpub. Sarah stepped aside to let them pass. Cullen did the same.

Sarah glanced at the door as if it were a black hole. "I'll make sure I don't embarrass you in front of your friends."

"You've never embarrassed me."

"What about the time I danced on the bar at the hole-in-the-wall dive near Joshua Tree?"

The taste of tequila shots with lemon and salt rushed back. He remembered how she'd moved to the pulse-pounding music. "I was turned on, not embarrassed, though I would have preferred a private performance without the other men leering at you. Then you could

167

have taken everything off—instead of only teasing with a couple of undone buttons."

"Well, then"—she flipped her hair behind her shoulder in a seamless, sexy move that nearly cut him to his knees—"I guess I have nothing to worry about tonight."

She might not, but Cullen couldn't say the same thing. He had a feeling he would be worrying for as long as Sarah was in town. Maybe even after she was gone.

Being out should have perked up Sarah's spirits and energized her like a toy bunny with brand-new batteries. But as soon as she stepped inside the brewpub, the smells of hops and grease assaulted her. Her stomach churned, not with hunger, but from a severe case of nerves.

Rock music played, but the din of conversation drowned out the lyrics. Servers dressed in jeans and black T-shirts carried pitchers of beers, pint glasses, and sodas.

"I see everyone," Cullen said.

Sarah had no idea how he'd found his friends so quickly, but she slowly followed him, weaving around crowded tables and past jam-packed booths, dodging people to keep them from running into her. She ignored the strong impulse to grab his hand.

That would be a bad move. Just like kissing him and coming here tonight. Sarah should have stayed at the cabin, locked away in her bedroom, where she wouldn't be so hypersensitive. Maybe her feelings were due to the aftereffects of his kiss or the anticipation of meeting more of his friends or…

Yours is a happy ending.

Yeah, that was what had gotten her panties—make that thong—in a twist and turned her insides into a quivering mess.

Sarah wanted a happily ever after of her own. Once upon a time, she thought she'd found hers with Cullen. But she should have known it wasn't meant to be. As a child, she had dreamed of living a storybook-type life, even when hers had been the antithesis of that, but she'd learned the chances of a happy ending were slim to none. The evidence suggested they didn't exist. She accepted that reality, though she hated the conclusion.

You were no longer a part of my life. I could start over in Hood Hamlet with a clean slate once the divorce was finalized.

She'd thought the same thing about living without him before her accident. Now she wasn't so sure.

Cullen had found the perfect place to spend the rest of his life, fall in love, get married again, and raise a family. She would go back to the institute, work until her grant was over, and then find another job somewhere else in the world. That adventurous way of life had always appealed to her.

Until now.

What was she thinking? She loved what she did. Work fulfilled her. Her job was her life.

The confusion, envy, and dissatisfaction had to be from the concussion and her injuries, tiredness, and hunger. Once she ate, she would feel better and the crazy thoughts would stop.

Cullen motioned to a long table. Attractive men filled one end while beautiful women sat on the other. "Most of the crew made it tonight."

Bill was with two men Sarah hadn't seen before. Cullen fit right in with that bunch of eye candy.

Zoe Hughes waved. She wore a colorful sleeveless shirt with ruffles on the front. A sparkly clip held her hair up with stylish, artfully placed tendrils around her face. "Leanne said we might see you tonight. I'm so glad you came."

Sarah wasn't used to people being so happy to see her. She liked how good that felt. "It took some convincing, but the good doctor finally relented."

Cullen raised his hands. "I know when to surrender."

Zoe's blue eyes twinkled. "Proud of you, Doc."

Introductions were made, and a pitcher of Jake's handcrafted root beer ordered for Sarah.

Leanne shooed him away. "Go sit with the guys, Doc, so us girls can chat."

Cullen pulled a chair out for Sarah. "Let me know when you're ready to eat. I'll go with you to the taco bar. It'll be difficult for you with one hand."

With a nod, she sat.

He pushed in her chair and then joined his friends.

Carly pushed her blond hair behind her ears. "Cullen

is so overprotective of you."

Leanne nodded. "I knew there was more to him than met the eye, but I never expected him to be so attentive."

"It's sweet." Zoe sighed. "I can't imagine how Sean would act if I was injured. I doubt he'd let me out of his sight or want me to do anything, either."

As if Cullen loved Sarah that much.

A lead weight settled in the bottom of her stomach. He might care, he might be concerned, but not in the way a devoted husband would be if something happened to his beloved wife.

Sarah glanced his way.

Tenderness filled his gaze.

Her heart bumped. Flustered, she angled away from him.

"You have more color than this morning." Leanne raised her glass. "Feeling better?"

Sarah might still be flushed from being so thoroughly kissed. Or it could be embarrassment. She cleared her throat. "Bill took me outside earlier for some fresh air."

"And now the brewpub." Carly sounded bubbly. "That's more excitement than you're used to."

Especially when Sarah added in Cullen's kisses. She nodded.

The server placed a pitcher of root beer and a glass on the table. Carly filled the cup and gave it to Sarah.

"Thanks." She took a sip. Thick and rich with the right amount of sweetness. "This is great."

Carly grinned. "Jake makes the best root beer in

Oregon."

"The two of you are so cute," Leanne teased. "You act like newlyweds, even with a baby."

"Nicki is officially a toddler now." Carly smiled at Jake. The two had done that a lot since Sarah sat at the table. The same with Sean and Zoe.

An engagement-ring-sized lump lodged in Sarah's throat. These happy couples gave her hope some marriages could succeed. They were also a harsh reminder of how hers had failed.

How did some people get so lucky? That was what she wanted to know.

A plate with two large pretzels and two small bowls containing mustard and cheese dipping sauces appeared in front of her. She peered over her shoulder to see Cullen standing there.

He smiled. "You wanted to try a pretzel."

His gesture touched her. If only they could have been one of the lucky couples. "I do."

"The pretzels are almost as good as the root beer." Carly grinned. "Of course, I'm biased."

Zoe flipped her hair. "The pretzels are better."

"Try one," Cullen urged.

"Listen to the good doctor." Leanne stared over the lip of her glass. "He would never lead you astray."

No, he had only flipped Sarah's world inside out by making her believe happy endings were possible. She took another sip of her root beer.

Cullen held a piece of pretzel in front of her face.

Mustard covered one end. "Open up."

The lump in her throat doubled. She glanced back.

A devilish grin curved his lips. "You know you want it."

Her heart slammed against her chest. She faced forward. This felt like…flirting.

As he brought the pretzel closer, she looked his way again. Wicked laughter lit his eyes.

She parted her lips, cautiously biting off the end of the pretzel. The bread, salt, and mustard sauce complemented each other perfectly. But she was more interested in Cullen's expression. He seemed to want a taste of her.

"How's the pretzel?" Jake asked.

The pretzel. Right. She focused on the men at the far end of the table. "Delicious."

But not as yummy as Cullen.

Her pulse picked up speed, accelerating as if she were tumbling downhill. Which was what she'd be doing if she didn't stop acting like a lovesick teenager. She turned away to find Zoe, Leanne, and Carly staring at her with rapt interest.

Sarah sipped her root beer, understanding their curiosity. Cullen feeding her was something a man who was part of a couple would do. She had no idea what was going on. Wasn't sure she had the strength to find out. Kissing him had been bad enough. Getting her hopes up and then discovering this was yet another fantasy would hurt worse than being hit by another steam blast.

No, thank you.

Chapter Fourteen

On the drive home from the brewpub, Sarah closed her eyes. The evening had taken its toll, physically as well as emotionally. Seeing Carly and Jake Porter and Zoe and Sean Hughes together made Sarah realize how far apart she and Cullen were and always had been. She sighed, not one of frustration but of resignation for what would never be.

The engine stopped. She opened her eyes.

The porch light illuminated the path through the darkness to the cabin's front door. The night was playing tricks on her vision. The distance appeared farther than it was. Too bad that wasn't the case with the separation between her and Cullen.

"Tired?" Cullen sounded concerned.

Despite the shadows in the truck's cab, the worry on his face was clear. Maybe that was part of the problem. His acting as if he cared what happened to her made their situation tougher to handle.

Cullen is so overprotective of you.

Too bad he was the same way with everyone he knew and strangers, also. "I'm a little tired."

She wasn't exhausted, but tiredness gave her an excuse to go straight to her room. No reason to linger and wish for what might have been or a goodnight kiss.

Sarah climbed out of the truck and hurried to the front door.

Cullen followed at her heels. "Slow down."

Sarah didn't. She couldn't. The happy couples tonight were too much of an in-her-face reminder of what she lacked. Insecurities from the past swamped her.

The women she'd sat with tonight were different from her. She would never have the perfect kind of wedded and domestic bliss the others had achieved. She could never be a perfect, proper wife. She wasn't made that way.

He unlocked and opened the door.

Sarah stepped inside, ready to retreat to her room, but his hand touched her shoulder. She nearly jumped.

"Let's sit for a minute." Cullen stood so close she could smell him, musky and warm and inviting.

The ache in her stomach increased. "Can't this wait until morning?"

"No." He led her to the sofa. "It won't take long."

Of course it wouldn't. Cullen never wanted to talk. The times she'd needed to talk to him, he'd retreated, upsetting her more. She didn't want to do the same thing to him, so she took a seat.

He sat next to her. "You seemed to have fun tonight."

She nodded. "Your friends are nice."

"They like you," he said. "Especially Paulson."

Sarah blew out a breath. "Bill's harmless."

"As harmless as a howitzer tank and about as subtle."

That made her smile.

"I'm glad you talked me into going." Cullen stretched his legs. "Seeing you with everyone tonight. Laughing and joking. It's as if you've been a part of the group forever."

Sarah stiffened. "What do you mean? Your friends are so…domestic."

"Paulson isn't."

"*Domestic* isn't right." She backtracked. "What I mean is they're caretakers. They watch out for each other. All for one. I'm more of an…adventurer."

"Your research will save lives in the future. I don't know how much more of a caretaker you could be."

Cullen was wrong. "I'm a loner, not the family type. Nothing like Carly, Zoe, Leanne, and Hannah. Or your mother and sisters…"

"What about my mom and sisters?"

Oops. Sarah hadn't meant to say that aloud. "It's nothing."

"Let me be the judge of that."

"It's just…" Sarah rubbed her mouth. "Well, it was obvious at Easter your family didn't like me."

Cullen flinched as if she'd slapped him. "That's not true."

Sarah shrugged her good shoulder, but her gut instincts were one hundred percent correct. She wasn't proper wife material. At least not for their son and brother. "It is. The way your family acted… I've never felt so inadequate in my life. And that's saying something after being dumped on my wedding day."

He made a face. "Come on."

The disbelief in his voice set her nerves more on edge. She hadn't fit into his family's out-of-this-world holiday celebration. They'd pushed her aside like the outsider she was.

"I wanted to help with dinner and tried," she explained. "But I only got in their way. They kicked me out of the kitchen and told me to find you."

"That's because they didn't want to put you to work. You were a guest."

"A guest." The word tasted like ash in her mouth. "I was your wife. I thought that meant I was family."

She'd wanted to be considered family. More than anything. But that hadn't happened. Their ready dismissal of her reaffirmed what she'd been trying to ignore—that she could never be the kind of wife Cullen needed. His parents and sisters would never accept her, and he wouldn't want her for much longer. Her dreams of finally being part of a loving family had died a painful death that day. So had her hopes for her future with him.

Tears welled. She blinked them away.

He started to speak but then stopped himself.

Sarah wasn't surprised he had nothing more to say.

She picked at the cast's padding around her fingers.

Cullen leaned toward her. "I should have told you. Warned you."

The regret, thick and heavy, in his voice shocked her. "About what?"

"Easter. My family. Blaine."

"What does your twin brother have to do with this?"

"Everything."

A chill slivered down Sarah's spine. Cullen's grief and sadness were as clear as they'd been that afternoon at Red Rocks when he'd mentioned his brother who had died. That was the one and only time he'd spoken of Blaine. She'd asked questions, but he'd never answered them.

She reached for his hand. His skin felt cold, not warm as usual. "You told me Blaine died when you were in college."

"He died on Easter."

Surprise washed over her. "On Easter Sunday?"

Cullen nodded. His hand wrapped around hers. Squeezed. "Blaine loved Easter. It was his favorite holiday. He always wanted more decorations and food. There were never enough eggs and candy for him. Because of what happened, my family goes all out on the holiday. Overcompensates."

She sat in stunned silence, angry he hadn't shared this information with her. Not telling her about breaking his arm as a kid was one thing, but this…

Easter weekend with the Grays had been the tipping point for her bringing up divorce.

"I…" A million thoughts swirled through her mind, but she didn't know where to begin. "I had no idea."

As Cullen scooted closer, his thigh pressed against hers. Self-preservation urged her to move away from him, but she hated that he was hurting.

His gaze locked on hers. "It's not just Easter. Over-the-top holidays and birthdays, especially mine, is my family's way of dealing with grief and the empty place at the table."

Easter hadn't been as perfect as she'd imagined—far from it actually. The realization sent her mind spinning. She tried to relate how she'd felt then with this new information.

His family had put on a good act. She'd never sensed what was going on beneath the surface. She'd been so focused on her own insecurities she hadn't wondered if there was a reason for *their* behavior. But she wasn't about to give Cullen a free pass over this. "You should have told me. I deserved to know. Do you realize I don't even know how Blaine died?"

"My brother was a drug addict." Cullen's voice cracked. "Blaine died of an overdose. I convinced myself it was accidental, but who knows? I found him unconscious in his bedroom when I went to get him for Easter dinner."

Horror flooded her. She gripped his hand, ignoring the urge to hold him. "Oh, Cullen. I'm so sorry."

"Me, too." Self-recriminations twisted his lips. "I failed Blaine. Interventions. Rehab. Tough love. My family… I tried everything, and I still couldn't save him."

Her heart ached for him and his family. "Addiction doesn't work that way."

"I know, but when it's your twin brother…"

"It's a horrible, impossible situation." Even knowing that, she couldn't imagine what Cullen had gone through when his brother was alive and afterward. Still, she wondered what else she might have misunderstood about him and his life. "If I'd known…"

It might have made a difference in their marriage. She could have understood why his family acted the way they had. She could have helped Cullen.

"I didn't want to burden you." He stroked her hand with his thumb. "I hadn't thought about how not knowing might affect you. You deserved to know, but being unable to help Blaine is my biggest failure. Talking about it to others is…difficult."

"I'm glad you told me now." Sarah waited for him to pull his hand away from hers. He didn't. Until he did, she would hold tight. She didn't want to break the connection with him.

This was the most open Cullen had been with her, and she feared he would shut down or run away from her again. She didn't want that to happen. "I'm sorry for not asking more questions about Blaine before, as well as not trying to understand your family's behavior."

"We both kept secrets from each other."

Sarah nodded. She hadn't told him about her ex-fiancé.

Cullen had hidden his pain the same way she'd hidden hers. She'd protected herself and her heart, never fully opening up to him because she hadn't trusted he'd stay in the relationship. No doubt he hadn't told her about Blaine because he'd felt the same way. Regrets grew exponentially until she struggled to breathe.

"We're quite the pair." Distrusting and afraid to let anyone in. Their marriage had never stood a chance without being open to each other—the kind of openness that would have allowed him to tell her the truth about his brother and family. The kind of openness that wouldn't have blinded her to Cullen's and his family's grief. "Holding back didn't help our marriage."

"No, but finally letting it all out feels good."

Seeing him open up reminded her of when they'd first met. He'd had no problem talking to her in Red Rocks. She'd wondered how he could have been so open there, but not when they returned to Seattle.

"Anything else you want to tell me?" Sarah tried to sound lighthearted. She wasn't sure she succeeded.

"There's nothing left to tell." His gaze raked over her. "Besides, you're tired."

Her chest tightened. She was losing him. He was retreating behind the doctor persona. But she wanted dearly to hang on to the moment. "I'm okay."

He pulled his hand away.

A deep ache welled within her soul. She missed his warmth. She missed…him.

"Your eyelids are heavy." He spoke in that

professional tone she was beginning to hate. "It's past time for your medicine."

Sarah stifled a yawn. Her long day *was* catching up to her, but she hated to let things end this way. "I can stay up a little longer. I'm feeling okay."

His gaze softened, not quite the look a physician gave a patient, but not one a loving husband gave to his wife. "The goal is to have you feeling better than okay."

Once she was better, she could return to Bellingham—except going back didn't appeal to her as it once had. Not when she wanted to recapture the closeness they'd just shared.

Every nerve ending screeched.

What was she thinking? Bellingham was where she belonged. She couldn't allow this moment—this *one* conversation—to change anything. That would be stupid.

Risking her heart again because he'd shown her a glimmer of what could have been would only hurt her in the end. Sarah had to stay focused on what was best for her. That was getting back to work. Her job wouldn't let her down.

She stood. "You're right. I'm more tired than I realized. I'm going to bed."

In the kitchen, Cullen washed his hands and then filled a

glass with water. He stretched his neck to each side but couldn't unknot his tight muscles.

His talk with Sarah hadn't gone as he'd expected. He'd wanted to know what she thought of his friends and the brewpub. He'd never planned on talking about Blaine. No one outside his family and close friends back home knew the truth, but Cullen had been compelled to tell her. He needed to rectify the mistake he'd made by not telling her about his brother. She'd needed to understand what had happened at Easter wasn't her fault.

He tore a paper towel off the roll and then dispensed her medications.

I've never felt so inadequate in my life.

The pain in those eight words, her tears gleaming, had been like daggers to his heart. Cullen hadn't wanted her to cry. She'd been hurt enough.

Because of him.

He'd wanted only to appease his family, particularly his mother, after missing the Easter before. Thanksgiving and Christmas, too. He hadn't considered Sarah's feelings during that trip home. He hadn't considered her much at all when they were together.

Except when they were in the bedroom.

That was the one place everything worked perfectly.

But it hadn't been enough. Not even close.

Expressing too much emotion equaled the loss of self-control, especially around Sarah, who had a way of tearing down his walls like no one else. But his silence—not talking and warning her how rough Easter would be for his family—had set her up for failure.

He couldn't undo the past, but he wanted to make it up to her somehow. Sarah had difficulty using her laptop and working for more than a few minutes. An idea formed…a way to help her do her job from the cabin. He could take care of that tomorrow.

Now, he wanted to make sure she hadn't overdone it today.

Cullen knocked on the closed bedroom door, careful not to spill any water. He didn't want Sarah to slip when she exited her room.

No answer.

He tried again.

Nothing.

A frisson of worry shot to the surface. He opened the door. "Sarah?"

She was lying in the center of the queen-sized bed, sound asleep. Her dark hair was spread across the pillowcase. She'd taken off her jacket and removed her boots, but she was still wearing the black yoga pants and red shirt.

I'm a little tired.

A little? Try a lot. Their discussion in the living room hadn't helped matters.

"Sarah." Cullen placed the water glass and medicine on the nightstand. He gently touched her good arm. "Wake up. You need to take your meds."

Her heavy eyelids cracked. "Must I?"

"You must."

With effort, she sat. "I thought you were a good doctor."

"I am, which is why you have to do this."

"I was sleeping fine without them."

"We want you to wake up feeling fine in the morning."

She blinked. "*We?* There hasn't been a *we* for a while."

"That's true." Cullen regretted contributing so much to that happening. "But we're here together now, and we both want you to recover."

Sarah nodded once, took the pills from him, and put them into her mouth.

He handed her the water.

She sipped and swallowed. "Thanks. I'm going to sleep."

"After you undress."

Sarah rested her head against the pillow. "I'm too tired."

Sleeping in her clothes would be uncomfortable, but she was an adult. Controlling Sarah never was something he'd wanted or tried to do. He wanted only to control her influence on him.

"Want help?" he offered.

Her eyelids fluttered. "Please. My pants. If you wouldn't mind."

Mind? He wasn't sure what he felt, but this seemed a light penance for his wrongdoings with her.

His fingers trembled with anticipation and need. He

touched her waistband.

Get a grip, Gray.

This had nothing to do with sex. He wanted to help her, if only to make amends for what he'd put her through during their marriage. But the crazy push-pull of regret versus the physical attraction was giving him whiplash.

Cullen pulled down the yoga pants. Glimpsing a patch of pink lace, he jerked his hand away.

They might be soon-to-be divorced, and she might be the last woman in the world he should want to be with, but that did nothing to lessen her appeal. His reaction had nothing to do with being celibate for so long.

It was Sarah.

No one else had ever made him feel this way.

He liked that. Liked how she'd held his hand as he talked about his twin brother. Liked how she trusted him to help her despite his failures.

"No problem. I've got this," she mumbled.

Suck it up, Gray.

Any fool could see she was exhausted. He needed to think about her—not himself. "Sleep. I'll take care of it."

That was the least he could do.

Cullen pulled the waistband over the curve of her hips and down her thighs. His hand grazed her skin. Sparks arced through his fingertips with each brush, but he managed to slide off the pants.

Sarah lay on the bed. Her eyes closed. Her lips parted.

He wondered what she dreamed about.

Him?

If only…

Cullen wanted to crawl into bed next to her and hold her, not only until the sun came up, but…forever. He yearned for the future he'd dreamed of having with her.

Even if she wanted the same thing, he might not be the best thing for her. He didn't know how to be more open. Showing his emotions unleashed the fear of losing himself. Talking about serious issues was plain torture. But maybe with Sarah's help, he could learn….

Chapter Fifteen

Something warmed Sarah's face. She opened her eyes. Sunlight flooded the room through the open blinds. Usually she closed them before she went to bed, but last night hadn't been the same as the ones before.

Cullen had opened up to her in a way she'd never expected.

What did that mean going forward?

She'd hoped something positive, but he'd given her medicine and removed her yoga pants. No goodnight kiss or peck on the forehead.

Sarah had been…disappointed. She chalked up her reaction to exhaustion. The last things she needed were any more kisses. Yet, this morning she was fighting a weird push-pull where Cullen was concerned.

She shrugged on her robe, tied the strap as best as she could, and headed out of her room. Would Hannah, Leanne, or Zoe be here this morning? Sarah had a feeling Bill wouldn't be back.

She entered the living room.

Bill held on to a ream of paper. "Good morning."

She did a double take. "You're babysitting me today?"

"Nope, I am." Sitting on the floor next to a leather recliner, Cullen worked on a printer.

Sarah scanned the living room: cords, boxes, the chair, and a table she'd never seen before. "What's going on?"

Bill grinned as if he'd eaten three canaries and two parrots. "You know how your head hurts and arm aches when you work on your laptop?"

She knew the feelings all too well. "Yes."

"Well, we had a great idea—"

"We?" Cullen asked.

The firefighter winked. "Doc had the idea to set up a comfortable workstation for you."

"You can print pages if the screen gives you a headache." Cullen tapped the printer.

She covered her mouth with her left hand. "This is…"

"Not exactly the definition of *fun,*" Cullen said.

"It's perfect." She studied the oversized recliner. "Where did the chair come from?"

He motioned his head toward Bill. "Paulson is good for a few things."

"A lot of things, if you happen to be a lovely lady." Bill ran his fingertips along the buttery leather. "This is my favorite chair. It's yours while you recover."

"Thank you." She hoped they knew how much this meant to her. "Thank you both. But you shouldn't have gone to so much trouble."

Cullen stood. "You need more to occupy your time than sleep, taking walks, and seeing doctors. Analyzing data will only hurt if you overdo it."

Sarah couldn't believe he'd listened and done something about what she'd said. Her heart swelled with joy. He kept surprising her each day. Maybe Cullen *had* changed. "I can't wait to work."

He brushed his hands together. "Breakfast first."

"What are we having?" Bill asked.

"Omelets and bacon, but I need to run to the store for more eggs."

"I'll go," Bill said and then took off.

She wanted to kiss Cullen and not only out of gratitude. Her heart lodged in her throat. "Thank you."

"Your job's important. This will make working easier on you."

And be the perfect distraction. She needed something to keep her from throwing herself into his arms and smothering his gorgeous face with kisses. "Are you working tonight?"

"Nope." He positioned the printer. "I'm caught up on the shifts I missed. I got lucky."

From Bill's chair to the table with the printer, Cullen had set up everything on the left-hand side. A rush of affection infused her. "I feel lucky myself."

Last night, everything in her world had seemed

wrong. Today it felt oh so right. Sarah couldn't believe Cullen had gone to so much trouble.

"Having me here can't be easy, but I appreciate what you've done and what you're doing." She couldn't change the past, but she spoke from the heart now. Today, Cullen was her Prince Charming, and she felt like a princess. Albeit a bruised and battered one, but a princess nonetheless. This might be the closest she ever got to a happy ending. "I hope you know that."

A satisfied smile settled on his lips. "I do now."

Over the next week, Sarah slept less and worked more. Interpreting data gave her a sense of purpose and kept her from thinking about Cullen. Okay, thinking about him *too much*. She still dreamed about him, but that was better than real-life kisses.

No matter how much living a fairy tale appealed to Sarah, she wasn't buying into the myth again. Others shared true love's kiss and found a happily ever after. Not her. She needed to stay focused.

Being with Cullen made her forget her goal wasn't to settle into a comfortable routine here. She forced herself to remember. There'd been room for her at his cabin but not in his life. A few conversations didn't make up for the times he hadn't wanted to talk. His kind gestures touched her, but they didn't change anything. She needed to return to Mount Baker where she could work and get back to *her* life.

And that was what she intended to do.

Today was her first day alone, a big step on her road to a full recovery. She was enjoying the independence. Oh, she'd missed the smell of coffee, breakfast, and conversations with her new friends. But she needed to do this in order to go to Bellingham.

After eating lunch, Sarah downloaded files from MBVI's server. She studied a data stream her boss wanted her to check. The seismometer appeared to be working properly. She'd worked with enough of these squiggly lines to know the difference between ice movement and data glitches, but something didn't make sense. Magma shouldn't move without generating more specific seismic signals. At least, she'd never seen that before.

After opening a new tab on her browser, she checked a website listing the many earthquakes that occurred daily in the Pacific Northwest. She scratched her head. "What am I missing here?"

"Me?"

A bevy of butterflies took flight in her stomach. She'd missed him, even if she shouldn't.

As he came toward her, his aquamarine polo shirt affected the shade of his blue eyes, reminding her of Los Tenideros in Costa Rica's Tenorio Volcano National Park, where two different-colored rivers merged. She'd traveled there after receiving her PhD and before starting at MBVI. She'd hoped the trip would heal the wound of her broken marriage. Hadn't worked. She now wondered if anything could do that.

Seeing Cullen filled her with happiness. A part of her wanted to fling herself into his arms, which would be stupid. She remained seated.

His wide smile showed off straight white teeth. He was gorgeous. Even more so than usual.

She gripped her laptop. "I didn't hear you come in."

"That's what happens when you're concentrating."

His tone teased, but he was right. She'd lost herself in her work. "I may be trying too hard."

He stood next to her, peering over her shoulder. "Head hurt?"

His concern warmed her like a fleece blanket. All she'd wanted was to be special to him. But he cared about everyone's well-being, not just hers. That was one reason he'd become a doctor. He'd mentioned Blaine as the other. Cullen might not have been able to save his twin brother, but he was doing his best to save others.

"My head is fine." She motioned to her laptop. "The data is causing me problems."

"Wrong?"

"Data is data. It can't be wrong. But my interpretation might be off," she admitted. "Things are inconclusive. I have a suspicion I may have started with too many preconceived notions."

He leaned forward, putting his hand on her shoulder. His male scent wrapped around Sarah, heat enveloping her. "Why do you think that?"

Cullen sounded interested, as if he wanted to know her thoughts. Tenderness and affection exploded in her chest. She glanced at the graph, trying to ignore her racing pulse, the pooling of desire, and the longing for connection squeezing her tightly. "Well…"

The numbers and lines blurred.

She blinked.

Everything remained fuzzy. Her head didn't hurt. It wasn't her concussion. All she could think about, all she wanted to see, was…

Cullen.

Her heart pounded like the surf ramming against the coast of Hawaii's Big Island.

Oh, no. She was falling for him. Again.

Realization nearly bowled her over. Not quite the same explosive force of five hundred atomic bombs detonating like the Mount Saint Helens eruption, but enough to send a chunk of molten lava crashing to the bottom of her stomach to take up permanent residence there.

Sarah struggled to breathe. Whatever happened, she couldn't fall all the way. That would be catastrophic.

"Sarah?"

"I—I thought my gut instinct was correct." She forced the words past the constriction in her throat. "I've been studying data to support a hypothesis. Not analyzing the data with an open mind."

Similar to what she'd done falling for him.

He sat on the couch. "It's not too late to start over."

She nodded. "I'm sure I can remedy this."

Because she knew where she'd gone wrong. Tucker wanted her at the institute ASAP. He'd mentioned her return again during their phone call this morning. She should have taken off by now, but she'd stayed to try to rework the data so she wouldn't have to leave.

Talk about stupid. She could be the poster child for the movement.

"Sarah?"

"Sorry." If she weren't careful, he'd think she suffered another head injury. "I'm...frustrated."

She had a job to do. A responsibility to the institute. She'd messed up her analysis. Not to mention allowing her feelings for Cullen to...deepen.

"Hey, don't look so sad. It'll be okay." He touched her hand. "Cut yourself some slack. You're still recovering." His calloused thumb made circles on her skin, leaving a trail of heat and tingles. "You've been working too hard."

Not hard enough. Sarah had become too distracted. She'd disregarded known facts and allowed herself to be caught up in a fantasy. Time to stop daydreaming and focus on reality.

Cullen might not act the same as he had a year ago, but she hadn't changed. Even if he was willing to give marriage another shot, the outcome would be the same. He would abandon her like everyone else in her life.

Sarah had to be strong. She squared her shoulders.

"What are you doing home? I thought you would be at Timberline all day."

Amusement twinkled in his eyes. "Look out the window."

Big, fluffy snowflakes fell from the sky. "When did it start snowing?"

"A couple of hours ago," he said. "Hughes, Paulson, and Moreno are on the slopes now."

"Go join them." Maybe that would give her time to try to save face, do her job correctly, and get him out of her head and heart again.

Cullen continued to rub her hand. "I can do that another day. I wanted to see how you were doing."

A warm and fuzzy feeling trickled through her.

Pathetic.

Sarah should be immune to him, not reacting like a lovesick teen. She tilted her chin. "I'm doing well."

"Well, but frustrated."

He was part of her frustration. That gave her an idea. "You need a break."

"You're the one who needs time away from the data, so you can relax."

Time away from Cullen to clear her head. She closed her laptop. "Sounds good. I'll take a nap. Grab your board and join your friends."

"I have a better idea. Let's take a break together."

Her heart rate resembled the data she'd been examining. Inconsistent and all over the place. "Don't waste your free time on me."

"I'd rather enjoy it with you."

She melted. Sarah couldn't help herself. She should decline politely, but she couldn't. Not when her clamoring heart drowned out all sense of self-preservation.

Mischief, as worrisome as a ticking bomb, glinted in his eyes. "Are you up for checking out Main Street with me?"

Temptation exploded with enough force to do significant damage. She wanted to spend time with him. Be with him. She might regret this. Who was she kidding? She *would* regret this. But she didn't care. "Please."

With Cullen at her side, she was up for anything.

Chapter Sixteen

Half an hour later, Cullen strolled along Main Street with Sarah. A layer of snow clung to her black jacket and colorful wool beanie. The cold air turned her cheeks a cute pink. She was so pretty. Most importantly, she was starting to look healthy again.

Wide-eyed, she spun to see the shops and sights. Her excitement added a bounce to his step. "This was just what I needed."

"Doctor knows best." That was why he'd suggested getting out. Her health.

Yeah, right.

He'd been counting the hours—minutes—until he could be with Sarah. She was on his mind constantly when he was away from her. When he was with her, too. "I have a surprise for you."

She rose on her tiptoes. "I love surprises."

Seeing her upset earlier with a life-as-she-knew-it-was-over expression on her face had made him feel as if he'd failed her somehow. He was relieved she was acting more like her old self, up for fun and adventure with him. "You'll enjoy this one."

Friends greeted him from across the street. Cullen waved.

"Are you planning to stay in Hood Hamlet permanently?" Sarah asked.

"Yes," he said without hesitating. "My lease is up next month. I might sign another year lease or go month-to-month a while. I'm considering buying a place."

She did a double take. "That's a big step."

True, but owning a house had always been part of his plan. So had a wife and kids…. He glanced at Sarah. "I like living here. It's a buyer's market."

"Strike while the iron is hot."

"Not quite." Cullen had learned his lesson by rushing into marriage. He jammed his hands into his jacket pockets. "I need to do more research first."

"What if you miss out on the perfect house?"

He'd thought Sarah was the perfect woman, and their marriage hadn't worked out the way he'd hoped. But he didn't want to think about that failure today. "Then I'll wait for the next perfect place to come on the market."

"We're so different."

Understatement of the year. "We had some good times together in spite of our differences."

She nodded. "More good than bad."

If she believed that, then why had she asked for a

divorce?

Sarah had never said she didn't love him. She'd told him he deserved better. That he should find another wife who could give him all he wanted.

All what?

He'd only wanted her.

No, that wasn't correct.

He'd wanted her when he chose. Not when she was on his mind making him incapable of thinking about or doing anything else.

Cullen dragged his hand through his hair. He'd let her down in so many ways. Was it too late to fix what had gone wrong?

He had no idea how to bring up that topic. Especially out in public.

She glanced into the coffee shop. A customer exited. The scents of coffee and freshly baked cookies drifted out the open door. "No wonder everyone around here is so active. You need to burn off calories from all the delicious-smelling food."

Sarah had changed the subject. Cullen would play along. "You figured out our motivation. The more time we spend on the mountain, the more we can eat without guilt."

"When have you ever felt guilty about eating?"

"At the hospital. When you couldn't."

Sarah's gaze softened. "You're sweet."

Brothers and friends were *sweet*. He would have preferred *hot* or *sexy*. But maybe sweet was where ex-husbands fit in. He didn't much like either moniker. "Do you know where you want to settle?"

She shrugged. "I'm not sure I'm the settling type."

Not surprising. Sarah seemed to have a permanent case of wanderlust. When she'd moved into his apartment in Seattle, everything she'd owned fit in her car. "How much longer is your postdoc?"

"It's tough to say after the accident. My funding will last a few more months, then I'll have to find a new position. I'm thinking about applying to the Global Volcano Monitoring Project."

The word *global* raised the hairs on the back of his neck. "What's that?"

"A nonprofit group that sends scientists all over the world, particularly to third-world nations, to set up volcano-monitoring systems and teach locals how to use them."

A sense of dread took root in his stomach. "Sounds interesting. Important."

She nodded. "It would be great experience. I'd be able to do a lot of good."

"You would." So why did this sound like a bad idea to him? Maybe because he would never see her again. But they were getting a divorce. He wouldn't see her again no matter where she lived.

Cars passed by. Neighbors greeted one another. A woman pushed a baby stroller. A tourist stood in the middle of the street snapping photographs.

She glanced around. "I can see why you want to settle

here."

"Yeah." Hood Hamlet was where Cullen wanted to be. So why couldn't he stop thinking about Sarah living in some remote village in Central America?

When they'd reached their destination, he stopped and pointed to the wood plaque hanging from the building. "This is your surprise."

Sarah read the words written in gold script. "'Welton Wines and Chocolates.' Two of my favorite things."

"That's why I wanted to bring you here." Chocolate was the second-best way to get rid of Sarah's frustration. The first way was more fun but not possible. He opened the door. A bell tinkled, announcing their arrival. "After you."

Her eyes resembled exquisite emeralds. "Thank you."

He followed her inside. "You're welcome."

Warm air greeted Cullen, chasing away the cold. His mouth watered from the aromas of chocolate and wine. The atmosphere was comfortable yet not too casual. Zoe Hughes had helped with the interior design. Chocolate was displayed on one side. A wine bar was on the other. In the back were black tables and chairs.

"This could be a dangerous place," Sarah whispered.

Not half as dangerous as her. "Let me have your coat."

Her eyes widened. "We're staying?"

"This wouldn't be much of a surprise if we went home, would it?"

She grinned. "I like your style, Dr. Gray."

He wished she liked him enough to stick around. He hung their jackets on the hat tree by the door.

Christian Welton, a firefighter and Leanne's fiancé, shook his hand. "Good to see you, Doc."

"This is Sarah Purcell," Cullen said. "I want her to experience one of Owen's chocolate tastings."

"Great." The firefighter's easy smile widened. "I'm Christian Welton. Nice to meet you. Leanne's told me all about you."

Sarah's face brightened. "Your ears should be burning. She said you were smokin' hot, and you are."

Leave it to Leanne and Sarah to speak their minds.

Christian's cheeks reddened. "Leanne mentioned the two of you had a lot in common."

"You have no idea," Cullen said.

Sarah's lower lip shot out. "What's that supposed to mean?"

Christian's gaze met Cullen's in understanding. "It means you and Leanne keep us on our toes."

The bell on the door jingled. More customers entered.

"Take a seat." Christian motioned to the tables. "We're getting set up. The tasting will begin soon."

Cullen and Sarah sat at a small round table with a single red rosebud in a glass vase and a lit votive candle. The flame flickered. Romantic. He hoped she enjoyed this.

She sniffed the flower. "This is a lovely shop."

Yes, which didn't explain why she was frowning. Cullen had to ask. "You don't look so sure about that."

"I'm confused because I thought Christian was a firefighter."

"He is, but his family owns a winery in the Willamette Valley," Cullen explained. "Christian and his cousin Owen opened this shop together a few months ago. Owen is a chocolatier."

She brightened. "I hadn't heard about the winery."

The bell on the door rang again. More people entered the shop, including Jake and Carly Porter and Hannah and Garrett Willingham, who sat at a table together.

Sarah waved. "Do you want to join your friends?"

Cullen wanted her to himself. "This is fine."

Christian placed carafes of water, glasses, and small plates of crackers on each table. Next came paper place mats with squares numbered one through six and pencils for each taster. "Welcome to Welton Wines and Chocolate. Today we'll be doing a tasting with our chocolatier, Owen Welton Slayter."

Owen limped out through a pair of swinging doors. He was dressed in a white chef's jacket and gray pants. Thanks to his climbing accident in November, he wore a leg brace. "We'll be tasting six samples, starting with milk chocolate that has the lowest percentage of cacao and ending with our darkest, most complex one. Since we don't want anything to affect the taste of the chocolate or dull your taste buds, we've provided room-temperature water, as well as unsalted crackers to cleanse your palate between each sample."

"Is it a law all males must be attractive to live in Hood Hamlet?" Sarah whispered.

At least she still found him attractive. Cullen's chest puffed out. "You'll have to ask the sheriff."

As Christian placed chocolate samples on the place mats, Owen lectured about the history of chocolate, beginning with the Mayans and Aztecs and the journey to Europe.

"This is in-depth." Sarah sounded impressed.

"Only the best for you, Lavagirl."

Stiffening, she appeared startled.

Cullen understood her reaction. The words surprised him, too. But he meant them. She deserved the best. Somehow, he wanted to make that happen for her.

She opened her mouth to speak. "Cull—"

He touched his finger to her lips. So soft and smooth. Nothing like they'd been at the hospital. "Not now."

"Allow me to give you a few pointers about tasting chocolate," Owen said to the group. "Examine each sample. Look at the color and the texture. Smell it. Snap the square in half. Does it sound sharp and crisp, soft and quiet, or something in between? After you place a piece in your mouth, don't chew. Let the chocolate melt on your tongue so you can experience the flavors as they unfold. If you have any questions, just ask."

As Sarah glanced at the place mat, her brows lowered.

Cullen scooted his chair closer to her. He wanted her to enjoy this, not be tense and wary. "Let's have fun."

With a nod, she tasted sample number one, following Owen's instructions as if she were doing an experiment in the laboratory.

"What do you think?" Cullen whispered.

"This one is smooth, but I prefer a stronger chocolate."

He placed his arm around her chair. "Mark what samples you like so we'll know what to buy."

She tapped her pencil against the table. "Aren't you going to keep track of your favorites?"

Cullen didn't have to. He was eyeing her now. "I'll keep track, too."

Amusement shone on Sarah's face. "Then you'd better taste your first selection or you'll be playing catch-up for the rest of the session."

He popped the square into his mouth. "You're right. Not rich enough for me."

The next two had deeper flavors. Sarah drew a heart around the number three on her place mat.

He toyed with the ends of her hair, letting the silky strands slip through his fingers. She glanced up at him. He took her silence as permission to continue.

"For centuries, many have touted the aphrodisiac qualities of chocolate," Owen lectured. "Some scientists have tried to debunk this, while others have claimed it's a psychological effect. Feel free to test this by feeding someone at your table sample number four."

Sarah held a chocolate in front of him. "Do you want me…?"

Chapter Seventeen

"Yes." Cullen wanted Sarah more than he could say, but the chocolate would have to do for now. He parted his lips.

She sucked in a breath. Her fingers trembling, she brought the sample to his mouth.

He didn't know if she was nervous over him or because she was using her left hand. He hoped it wasn't the latter. He liked the idea she might be as affected by him as he was by her.

She carefully placed the chocolate onto his tongue. "What do you think?"

The intense flavor burst in his mouth with a nutty and buttery taste. The third sample had been more velvety with a hint of orange.

"Delicious." He picked up the fourth piece off his place mat. "Your turn."

Something resembling panic flashed across her face, but she opened her mouth. He brought the chocolate closer. The tip of her tongue came out. Cullen fed her the sample.

Sarah's lips closed simultaneously with her eyes.

The aphrodisiac effects of chocolate might not be quantifiable, but he was feeling something. When she opened her eyes, the desire flaring in her gaze suggested she was feeling it, too.

He wanted to kiss her. Instead, he scribbled a star next to the number four on his place mat. "We're buying this one, too."

When he glanced at Sarah, the tip of her tongue darted out once again and licked her lower lip.

Cullen wanted a taste. He leaned closer and kissed her. Gently.

She tensed before relaxing and kissing him back. He pressed his lips more firmly against hers, enjoying the warmth, the sweetness, and the touch of spice that was uniquely Sarah. As with the chocolate samples, the flavors unfolded one after another.

Her kiss filled the loneliness in his heart. He'd missed her so much. Not in a negative, obsessive way as he'd feared would happen, but as one person who loved another and wanted to be with them. He didn't want her to go to Bellingham or anywhere else. He wanted her to stay with him as his wife.

"Let's move on to sample five," Owen said.

Cullen drew back, even if he would have rather skipped the rest of the tasting and continued kissing her. Sarah's confused expression tugged at his heart.

He'd kissed her—been with her a large chunk of the day. And he hadn't felt himself losing control. If anything, he was finding himself. He wanted to make things right between them and be a better husband.

He marked his place mat with the pencil. "I'm going to want another taste of number seven."

Her eyebrows bunched. "There are only six samples."

"Seven, if I count you."

She smiled shyly, peeking at him through her eyelashes.

He leaned closer. "I have a strong feeling number seven is going to be my favorite."

Gratitude glistened in her eyes. Something else, too. Something resembling...hope. "Mine, too."

As the tasting continued, Cullen forced himself to concentrate. All he wanted to do was stare at Sarah and kiss her again. Not in that particular order. But she was paying attention to Owen, so Cullen reluctantly did as well, while wondering how he could keep things between them moving in the right direction. Not only today, but...forever.

Number five was delicious—hints of sugary coconut—and went on the to-buy list. Number six was too bitter.

As the tasting came to an end, people discussed their observations. Everyone liked something different about the samples.

Cullen rubbed her back. "Enjoying yourself?"

"What are we doing?"

"Tasting chocolate."

"I mean…" She glanced around as if to see if anyone was listening. "You're acting as if we're…"

"What?"

"Married."

"We are."

"For now." She glanced over at the table where his friends sat. "But you're doing all this lovey-dovey couple stuff. I'll be honest. I'm enjoying it. But your friends have noticed. What are they going to think?"

She enjoyed it. Good. Him, too. He didn't want the lovey-dovey stuff, as she called it, to end. "I don't care what they think."

"You said you told them about us."

He nodded. "They know I filed for divorce."

Sarah's face paled. "You filed?"

Her shocked tone made him feel like a jerk. He moved his hand off her but kept his arm on her chair. "I mentioned I'd gotten things started when you were at the hospital."

She nibbled on her lip. "I'm sorry. You did, but I hadn't realized that meant you'd filed."

Okay, he was confused. What else would starting a divorce proceeding mean?

"No big deal who filed, right?" Except when all he wanted was to kiss her, maybe he'd been premature in setting the divorce into motion. "I hope you're not upset."

"Not upset." A mannequin would have a more natural expression. "I wasn't clear on what you meant. Must be the concussion."

"Probably." But doubts clamored to the surface. Hope spread. In a flash, dreams and plans he'd suppressed surged to the forefront of his mind. His heart battered against his rib cage. "One call to my lawyer will stop everything. Unless you still want a divorce."

As soon as he'd spoken, he was afraid to hear her answer. What if she said yes? What if she said no? With her life in Bellingham and his in Hood Hamlet, divorce was the logical choice, but his heart no longer agreed with his head about that.

It was taking her a long time to answer. Too long.

Cullen stood, disgusted with himself for thinking they might stand a chance. "I'm going to buy some chocolate while you think about it."

Unless you still want a divorce.

If today was the benchmark for the future, then no, Sarah didn't. She tapped the pencil so fast against the table she might as well have picked up Cullen's and performed a drum roll. But one day didn't make a marriage. Nor did two, the amount of time they'd spent together before eloping.

Even if things went well, how long would it be before

Cullen changed his mind, realizing he could do better or got tired of her?

She dropped her pencil. Probably not long.

The sooner she got out of here, the better.

And she didn't mean this shop.

Grinning, Carly approached the table. "It's so good to see you and Cullen here."

Hannah joined them. "I can't believe how much better you look. You're glowing."

"Thanks." Sarah didn't want to talk with *Cullen's* friends, each who knew more about her marriage—make that the *end* of her marriage—than she did. But these women had become her friends, too. She could smile at them. And did. "The doctor's pleased with my progress."

Carly winked. "The good doctor seems very happy."

"The two of you look great together." Hannah's face lit up. "Seems like more is healing than your injuries."

Sarah pressed her toes into the floor so hard she was sure she'd made a hole. She understood these two women believed in a forever kind of love. They meant well, but she didn't know how to answer them. "Anything can happen."

She hoped that satisfied them.

Hannah nodded. "Especially here in Hood Hamlet."

"Christmas magic in June." Carly beamed.

"Magic doesn't exist." Sarah didn't care what Cullen had said on their drive to Hood Hamlet. "It's nothing more than an illusion."

The two women shared a glance.

214

"Of course you feel that way. You're a scientist," Hannah said. "But after you've been in Hood Hamlet for a while, you'll change your mind."

Carly nodded. "It happens to everyone. Including Cullen."

No way. This was too woo-woo for her analytical brain. Magic no more existed than everlasting love did.

A good thing. She couldn't allow herself to be lured in by any yearning, whether that meant believing in magic or in love or in a happily ever after. "I won't be in town long enough for that to happen."

"Cullen doesn't seem ready for you to leave yet," Carly said.

Hannah glanced at him as he stood in line at the chocolate counter. "You have more healing to do."

"I do." But that wouldn't change Sarah's beliefs. She was a scientist grounded in fact. She had to stand firm. If she wasn't careful, if she allowed herself to believe, her heart could be obliterated.

She wished Cullen would hurry so she could escape the scrutiny of his friends. But he was engrossed in a conversation with Jake, Garrett, and Christian.

Cullen's happiness did painful things to her stomach that had nothing to do with her surgical incision or broken ribs. She struggled to breathe.

What was going on? The man had filed for divorce, and he still affected her this way? *A divorce she'd brought up*, a little voice taunted.

Regret assailed her.

She focused on the two women, who hadn't missed the exchange. Their enthusiastic smiles suggested they might think the divorce had been put on the back burner.

Sarah opened her mouth to clarify things, but she didn't know what to say.

This surprise outing was becoming a nightmare. She wanted to go home—strike that, to the cabin—and hide away in her—the guest—bedroom until he went to work or on a mission.

As Cullen moved toward her, he held up a white bag with gold lettering. "I've got the chocolate."

Good. Sarah could scarf down the entire bag once she was in her room. She stood, eager to escape this place.

"I don't know if you have dinner plans for tonight, but we'd love for you to join us," Hannah said, much to Sarah's regret. "Jake and Carly are coming over with Nicole, so this will be a kid-friendly menu. Nothing fancy, just lasagna."

Cullen glanced at her. "Sarah loves lasagna."

She was touched he remembered but annoyed he'd bring it up now. She forced a feeble smile.

"I'm bringing dessert," Carly added.

"What do you say, Sarah?" he asked.

He'd given her the choice. Sure, she had an easy out if she said she was tired. People would understand. Too bad she was confused, wary, and apprehensive— everything but tired. How could she lie to a woman who had done so much to care for her? "Sure, sounds fun."

As much fun as more surgery.

Hannah grinned. "Great."

Yes, great. At least, Hannah was happy. Sarah's face muscles hurt trying to keep her panic from showing, but her smile never wavered. She had a feeling this would be a long evening. At least she had Carly's dessert to look forward to at the end. There was, however, one bright spot ahead—she wouldn't be spending the evening alone with Cullen.

She tugged on her ear. Maybe dinner out wasn't such a bad idea after all.

Chapter Eighteen

"The lasagna tasted great, Hannah." Cullen enjoyed being at the Willinghams' house. Nothing like sitting at a crowded dinner table with good friends, tasty food, and his beautiful wife. His arm rested on her chair. The ends of her hair tickled his skin. He could get used to this. "Thanks for inviting us over."

"Everything was delicious," Sarah agreed. Jake and Carly chimed in with praise, too.

Cullen's thigh touched Sarah's. He thought about shifting positions to break the contact, but she wasn't scooting away. Might as well stay put, even if his blood simmered.

He wished it could always be like this with Sarah. Hanging out with friends. Kids running around.

They hadn't gone out with other couples in Seattle. With such busy schedules, they'd kept to themselves, spending any free time with each other. Maybe that had been a mistake.

Hannah wiped the mouth of her two-year-old son, Tyler. The boy squirmed and scrunched his face. She didn't miss a beat. "Do you want dessert now or later?"

"Later," the adults said at the same time.

"Then let's go into the living room." Hannah stood. "Cleanup can wait."

Garrett leaned over and kissed his wife. "I'll take care of the kitchen for you."

Her older children—Kendall and Austin—bolted from the table. Tyler and fifteen-month-old Nicole, Jake and Carly's daughter, toddled after them, nearly crashing into each other twice.

Carly laughed. "At least diapers provide padding when they fall."

The adults followed the kids into the living room, spreading out to take seats on the worn but comfortable furniture. Pieces from a jigsaw puzzle covered the coffee table. Crayons and LEGO bricks lay scattered on the floor.

Cullen wanted to buy a house similar to this one. Warm and cozy, well-built, and designed for a family. But his dreams had always included Sarah. Never any other woman, only her.

She sat on the couch with Carly.

He wished Sarah had sat by him on the loveseat instead.

The two women joked about something wedding-related.

He understood why Sarah had wanted to elope after

being jilted on her wedding day, but he'd never asked if she wanted a reception or a party to celebrate their marriage. They'd never taken a honeymoon, only short climbing trips. They'd never shared a bank account, either.

Framed photographs covered the fireplace mantel. The wedding pictures drew his attention. He and Sarah had two wedding photographs, one with the Elvis impersonator and one alone. It had seemed enough at the time. And too much when he'd been moving out.

Music played, a light jazzy instrumental song.

A picture of a climber standing atop Mount Hood with a big grin on his face caught Cullen's attention. The gear dated the photo. That must be Nick Bishop, Carly's brother, Hannah's first husband, and Kendall and Austin's dad, who'd died in a climbing accident on Mount Hood.

The women laughed over something borrowed. Or was it blue?

Kendall, who was around twelve, carried in a cardboard box and set it at Sarah's feet. "My mom says you're a volcano scientist."

"I am," Sarah said enthusiastically. "At Mount Baker Volcano Institute. My specialty is seismology."

The girl's face fell. "Bummer. I need someone to help me who knows something about lava flow."

The corners of Sarah's mouth twitched, but she kept a serious expression on her face. "I know something about lava. What do you need help with?"

"My science-fair project."

Hannah touched her daughter's thin shoulder. "Sarah is a guest. Let's not bother her with your homework."

Kendall shrugged away from her mother's hand. "But you and Dad know nothing about volcanoes."

"I'm happy to help," Sarah said, much to Cullen's surprise, given her pensive mood and how inexperienced she seemed to be around kids. "I've given talks at schools and led geology field trips around Mount Baker."

As Kendall dug through the box, Hannah mouthed *thank you* to Sarah. Austin showed Jake his newest handheld video game. Carly played peek-a-boo with Nicole and Tyler.

Sarah gave Hannah a quick nod before focusing on Kendall. "Let me see what you have."

The girl showed her the jam-packed box—maps, a plastic bucket, and other items Cullen didn't recognize.

"You've got plenty of supplies to make a project." Sarah surveyed the contents, picking something up to examine more closely. "Is there a quieter place where we can work?"

"Yes. I know just the place." Kendall, all limbs and hair, scrambled to her feet. "Follow me."

As Kendall jogged out of the living room carrying her box with her little brother Tyler chasing after her, Sarah stood. "How much help is Kendall allowed to have with the project?"

"She's supposed to do the majority of the physical

work herself," Garrett said. "But she can have as much assistance as needed with the concepts and science behind the project."

"Got it," Sarah said.

"Tyler went with Kendall. If he's in the way, let me know," Garrett added.

Sarah waved her hand. "No worries. We'll find something for him to do."

Her willingness to help surprised Cullen, given her awkwardness with his nephews and nieces that Easter. Maybe spending more time with kids on field trips had made a difference. He remembered what she'd said to him during their conversation in his living room.

I wanted to help with dinner and tried. But I only got in their way. They kicked me out of the kitchen and told me to go find you.

Had his family treated Sarah the same way when she'd wanted to help with the kids? Granted, they hadn't been happy when he'd eloped because they worried his behavior had been too reckless. No one wanted him following in Blaine's footsteps. But surely his family wouldn't have taken their concerns out on Sarah.

Except that was what he'd done. He'd blamed Sarah for his impulsive behavior in Las Vegas. Even though marrying her had made him feel better, happy, complete.

Hannah stared down the hallway. "Sarah doesn't have to do this."

"She knows that," Cullen explained. "But given the choice between volcanoes and doing something else, she'll pick volcanoes every time."

But his words didn't quite ring true. She'd had research to do for her dissertation and other obligations at the university. But she'd worked around his schedule as much as possible. He hadn't felt like a priority because he hadn't wanted to be one. He'd wanted her to be busy so he had a reason to be, too.

Busy equaled distracted.

He rubbed his neck.

Carly picked up Nicole. "You know, the USGS Cascade Volcano Observatory isn't that far away."

Jake held a bottle of beer. "Vancouver, Washington, isn't exactly close."

"It's closer than Bellingham, where Sarah works now," Hannah countered.

Garrett shot his wife a pointed look. Something Cullen hadn't expected from the button-downed CPA who was also OMSAR's treasurer. "Drop it."

Jake nodded. "You, too, Carly. Doc doesn't need you interfering in his life."

"Especially his marriage," Garrett added.

"What? We haven't done anything." Hannah raised her palms. "Carly and I thought we'd mention it in case Cullen and Sarah want to be closer."

Closer, huh?

The muscle cords in Cullen's neck tightened. Sarah had been right. His friends had noticed them at the chocolate tasting and had made their own assumptions. Wrong ones. Though a part of him wished they were correct. Sarah had never answered his question about still wanting the divorce. "Sarah and I aren't back together."

"Not yet anyway." Carly spoke as if she knew a big secret. "Anyone can see the two of you are perfect together."

He'd thought that once himself. Now…

Jake blew out an exasperated breath. "Be careful, Doc, or you'll find these two playing matchmaker."

Hannah placed her hands on her hips. "We aren't that bad."

"That's because you haven't been given the chance." Garrett shook his head. "They mean well, Doc, but don't let them get away with anything or you'll have an avalanche on your hands."

Cullen gave both men a nod. He stood. "Appreciate the warning, gentlemen. I'm going to see how the science project is coming along."

And get out from under the would-be-matchmaking reach of the ladies.

"Just follow the sounds of wailing and gnashing of teeth and you'll find Kendall," Hannah said.

Carly made a sour face. "Hey, that's my niece you're talking about."

"Wait until Nicole is twelve." Hannah sighed. "You'll understand. I can't imagine what it'll be like when Kendall turns thirteen."

Cullen left them to discuss teenagers. Heading down the hallway, he didn't hear wailing, but a few giggles and squeals pierced the quiet. He followed the sounds until he came to a garage.

He stood in the doorway.

Sarah sat in a camp chair. The two kids were on the concrete floor with the contents of the box spread out in front of them. Tyler played with an empty paper towel roll. He couldn't seem to make up his mind whether the cardboard was a sword or a bugle.

"This is going to be so cool." Kneeling, Kendall leaned forward. "If it works."

"It'll work." Sarah pointed to a piece of paper on the floor. "You need to attach this onto the topographic map."

"Like this?" the girl said shyly.

Sarah gave Kendall the thumbs-up sign. "That's perfect."

Tyler mimicked the action.

Grinning at the little boy, Sarah rubbed her hand over his hair. "You are too cute."

The boy stared up at her with pure adoration.

Cullen's heart stuttered.

As Tyler examined her cast, Sarah touched Kendall's shoulder. "You're doing an excellent job."

Kendall beamed. "That's because I have you."

"You're doing all the work." Sarah sounded like a mom.

Cullen couldn't breathe.

"I'm simply your scientific adviser," she added.

"Is it fun being a scientist?" Kendall asked.

Sarah's beaming smile hit Cullen like a blast from a laser gun. He leaned against the doorjamb to keep from falling over. Because the floor was the next place he'd be. No doubt about it.

"Being a scientist is the most fun job in the world." She explained what she did at MBVI.

Kendall held on to Sarah's every word. He didn't blame the girl. He reacted the same way.

"Is it better than being a wife and mom?" Kendall asked.

Sarah's tender gaze washed over the two children. "I don't have kids, so I don't know about that, but being a wife can be fun, too."

Cullen listened in disbelief, held spellbound by the woman he'd married. His life plan swirled inside his brain, reconfiguring and amending itself by the second.

Kendall fiddled with a piece of plastic. "I can use water for the lava."

"You could, but molasses would work better due to its viscosity."

"My mom has molasses in the pantry." Kendall stared up at Sarah. "But I'm not sure what *visc*…whatever you said means."

"Viscosity."

Kendall repeated the word. "Viscosity."

Sarah nodded. "Viscosity is the measure of a fluid's resistance to flow."

"Huh?"

"Imagine you have a cup of water and a cup of honey. Which drains faster?"

"The water. Honey moves slower."

"That's right," Sarah said. "Honey has a higher viscosity than water, so it resists flow more. Same with molasses."

"Makes sense."

As the two worked on the volcano, Cullen was captivated by how much Sarah had changed from being awkward and uncomfortable around his family at Easter to at ease with Tyler and Kendall.

This new side of Sarah appealed to him at a gut level. He pictured her with children of her own, nurturing them, mothering them. All the heady dreams he'd had when they'd first married rushed to the forefront of his mind. Sarah pregnant with his child. A girl with her laugh. A boy with her sharp wit. They would be a family.

His family.

Cullen's heart ached with yearning so strong his feet carried him toward Sarah. Until he realized she would be the mom of some other guy's kids.

He balled his hands.

Unless you still want a divorce.

She hadn't answered him but that didn't matter.

Forget pride. Forget everything.

Forget losing her. He wanted a second chance. How could he convince her to give their marriage another shot? What if she didn't want to try again?

His heart thudded. But what if she did?

Chapter Nineteen

Later that night, Cullen unlocked the front door of the cabin. "You were amazing tonight."

Sarah went inside. She wanted to be unaffected by him, yet all she wanted to do was kiss him. Giving in to her impulsive side wouldn't be smart with her heart at stake. "I didn't do that much."

"You only made a kid's night by helping her put together what will be the winning science project."

Sarah had never felt like such a part of a community, of a family, until tonight. She'd loved every single second of being at the Willinghams' house, from eating dinner to helping Kendall with her volcano model to hugs from Tyler with his always sticky hands. For the first time, Sarah wondered if she could be a good wife and mother despite her past.

Sadness trembled down her spine. Hood Hamlet wasn't her community and Cullen…

She swallowed a sigh. "Anyone would have helped."

"But you did."

She shrugged off her jacket. "I don't know why you're making such a big deal about this."

"The last time you were around kids, you looked like you wanted to run and hide."

Easter. The right sleeve caught on her cast.

Cullen removed it for her. He hung the jacket on the hat tree by the door. "Tonight was the antithesis of that."

Sarah crossed her arm over her chest and rubbed her cast. "Tonight was more real than Easter with your family."

With his hand at the small of her back, he led her into the living room. "Easter was real."

She sat on the couch, and he took a seat next to her. "Okay, you're right, but everything was scheduled with military precision. We moved from one activity to the next without having a chance to enjoy the moment. No opportunity to catch our breaths. No time to think about anything. I understand now that's the whole purpose of the holiday being so over the top. The day is jam-packed with so many things so Blaine doesn't have a chance to enter your minds."

Cullen rubbed his palms on his thighs as if drying them off. "I told you it's a coping mechanism."

"Yes. But remember, I hadn't a clue then." She needed to get this out, if only for her peace of mind. "All I saw were little kids who wanted to play with their Easter baskets and eat candy, not do crafts, be forced into organized games, and march in a parade. I mentioned it to your mom, and she snapped at me. Your sisters jumped all over me, too."

His nostrils flared. "Why didn't you tell me?"

"You never wanted to talk about anything." Sarah kept her voice low and steady, even though her emotions and stomach churned. "Why would that have been any different?"

"I…" He hung his head. "It's probably too late to apologize."

Sarah touched his hand; his skin was rough, calloused, and warm. "It's okay. Addiction does crazy things to people, and this is how your family deals with what happened to Blaine. But knowing the history going in would have saved a lot of heartache."

He nodded. "I'm not one for doing a lot of talking."

"You had no problem talking to me in Las Vegas."

"Vegas was different."

"Yes, it was." Those two days had been a fairy tale. But in the real world, they couldn't sustain the fantasy. "We could be what each other needed there. In Seattle, not so much."

His gaze darkened to a midnight blue. "That's—"

"The truth."

Cullen didn't say anything, but his chin dropped.

A nod of agreement? She couldn't be sure.

"We're doing better now," he said. "Talking. Trying."

"Yes, but this isn't real. I mean, I'm still recovering. It's almost like I'm on vacation."

"Like in Red Rocks."

Disappointment squeezed her heart. She nodded. "But you're not on vacation. You're home. I realized Hood Hamlet's true appeal to you tonight."

Cullen eyed her. "What's that?"

"The community, the people. They're one big extended family. You take care of one another and have each other's backs, like your sisters had your mom's with me. Or Leanne wanting to know about our marriage."

"Or Hannah and Carly mentioning the volcano observatory in Vancouver wasn't that far away."

Sarah inhaled sharply. "They didn't."

"They did." Cullen sounded amused. "Much to Garrett's and Jake's dismay."

"No wonder you found your way to the kids and me."

"I was afraid to stay in the living room any longer."

She laughed.

"Maybe I should have listened to what they had to say. Because they're right about one thing." He raised her hand to his mouth and kissed it. "You belong here."

Her heart stumbled.

"In Hood Hamlet," he continued.

Sarah thought he was going to say she belonged with him. Hoped he would. But he hadn't. She ignored the disappointment. "I live in Bellingham. MBVI is there."

"I live here." His gaze trapped hers. "We should be together."

The poles shifted. Her world spun off its axis. Air

rushed from her lungs. "Together?"

He nodded with a determined set to his jaw. "A couple."

Surprise clogged her throat. It took a second to find her voice. "We tried that."

"We didn't try hard enough." He took a breath. "I didn't try hard enough."

Her mouth gaped. She couldn't believe he was owning up to what happened.

"We're good together now. Better than we were in Seattle. That's a start to making us work."

Us.

If only… No. Too much separated them. Too high a wall to climb, too wide a river to cross. "We're so different."

A seductive fire blazed in his eyes. "Opposites attract."

He leaned closer. His heat enveloped her.

Feeling lightheaded, she forced herself to focus. "They can also repel."

One side of his mouth lifted in a sexy grin. "We definitely attract."

She struggled to breathe.

"I'll prove it to you." His lips swooped down on hers. He kissed her until her toes curled, sparks ignited under her skin, and she was gasping for air. "Enough of a data point, or do you need more?"

Oh, she had the information she needed to make a conclusion. That brief but oh-so-hot kiss reminded her of when they'd first met. His kisses had stripped her bare, leaving her emotionally vulnerable and wanting another kiss. All her dormant fairy-tale fantasies had clamored to be heard.

But Sarah didn't need to be rescued. She couldn't fall under Cullen's spell the way she had in Las Vegas. The way he'd—*they'd*—acted tonight made believing they could be a couple again so easy, not the same as before, but more like Hannah and Garrett or Carly and Jake. The way Sarah had always dreamed.

But how long would that last?

Her parents had abandoned her. So had Dylan, her ex-fiancé. Cullen had, too.

He hadn't fought for her. He hadn't even bothered to try.

She found it difficult—okay, impossible—to believe Cullen would stay the distance this time. And when he ditched her...

She couldn't let him make her believe in magic or happy endings. "I can't."

He stroked her cheek with his knuckle. "You're going to have to give me more than that."

That was what she was afraid he would say. "I'm tired."

He wrapped a finger around a loose curl. "We can have this conversation lying down."

Warning bells clanged in her head. "Cullen."

"Nothing wrong with the horizontal position," he said. "You used to enjoy it."

Loved it. Heat pooled low in her belly and spread outward, making her limbs feel like liquid silver. She swallowed.

"Come on." He pulled her up from the couch. Tugged her gently forward by a wayward curl. "Get ready for bed. Then you can tell me why you 'can't.'"

Can't. Can't. Can't. The word echoed through Sarah's head.

She took her time in the bathroom getting ready for bed. A mix of procrastination and nerves vied for victory. Except she didn't imagine there would be a winner tonight.

Apprehension coursed through her veins. She put on her robe over her pajamas. An extra layer of protection. Not from Cullen. From herself.

In her room, she crawled into bed and then pulled the covers to her neck. She willed herself to sleep. Impossible to talk if she was asleep.

Cullen entered the room wearing only pajama bottoms. His muscular arms, smooth chest, and defined abs made her mouth water. He looked as though he'd been sculpted to her specifications.

Her fingers itched to run over his skin, to feel his strength and warmth. She wanted his hands to touch her.

As Sarah shivered with need, he took a step toward

her.

"I'm not having sex with you." The words fell from her mouth like a glacier calving.

His lopsided, heart-stopping grin appeared again. "Who said anything about sex?"

The man was sex with a stethoscope. Well, if he had one around his neck. "Just setting the ground rules."

"That's rule number one. Any more?"

She narrowed her eyes. "Maybe."

Amusement curved his lips. He flicked off the light.

Darkness filled the room.

As he stretched out beside her, the mattress dipped.

She tightened her grip on the blanket. "Stay on top of the covers."

"Your wish is my command."

Sarah gulped. That was what she was afraid of.

He cuddled against her.

Every one of her muscles tensed. "What are you doing?"

"Getting comfortable for our conversation."

That would be impossible for her to do. Even with the covers, a robe, and pajamas separating them, warmth emanated from his body, flowing to hers. The heat felt good. So did he.

"Can you explain why we can't be together?" he asked.

"You're serious about having this discussion in bed?"

"You sound surprised." He, however, spoke in a

calm tone. "Did you think I was going to put the moves on you?"

"Yes." She'd hoped. Dreaded. And, well, she was about as confused as she could be right now.

He guffawed. "O, ye of little faith."

"I have only past experience to go by." She inhaled and then exhaled slowly. "That's why I can't be with you. I'm no good at relationships. And neither are you."

Sarah expected him to offer up a counterpoint. He didn't. The crushing weight of disappointment settled on her chest.

The house creaked. The heater came on, shooting warm air through the vents. Outside, the wind blew.

"I'll admit I failed the first time around, but that doesn't mean I can't do better the second." He brushed his fingers through her hair. "Why do you think you're not good at them?"

She doubted he wanted to stay up all night to hear the long list of reasons. Might as well cut to the chase. "I haven't told you much about my parents."

"You said they've each been divorced multiple times and they're no longer part of your life."

Thinking about the last time she saw her mother still hurt. "I was an only child, and my parents should have never had me. I think they regretted it. But one thing was clear. They didn't care about me."

"What do you mean?"

"They never wanted me around. After the divorce, they shuttled me back and forth."

He pulled her closer. "That's no way to treat a child."

"No, but that's what they did." The numb tone of her voice matched the way she felt. Resigned. Indifferent. That was how she wanted to feel about what had happened. "I've never seen or experienced a successful relationship. Only broken ones."

"You saw two tonight at dinner."

"A glimpse." She shivered, and his arms tightened around her. "Being jilted and having my parents walk away has skewed my view."

What happened with Cullen was the final data point. She didn't need any more.

"You don't have to tell me."

"I want to." She should have told him long ago. "I wanted you to talk to me, but I wasn't so eager to do the same myself."

"We share the blame. I didn't ask you a lot of questions," he admitted. "So your folks…"

"My mom's fourth husband made a pass at me. It had happened before with men she was dating, so I always made myself scarce, but I'd never had one of my stepfathers do that before."

Cullen brushed his lips over her hair. "I'm sorry it had to happen at all."

"I told my mom because I was scared, but my stepfather lied. Claimed I was trying to seduce him. My mom believed him. Kicked me out of the house. I was heartbroken, humiliated…you name it."

The memory burned through her.

"Shame on your mom. That's horrible choosing a man over her own daughter." He squeezed her. "Did you go live with your dad?"

"Yes, but I bounced around a lot. I was in high school. I ended up spending a lot of time with Dylan."

"You were with him a long time."

She nodded. "He was all I had. My dad's new wife, Caylee, was uncomfortable having a stepdaughter who was five years younger than her. I petitioned to be emancipated when I was seventeen. After that, I never saw my dad again."

"Sarah—"

"It's okay. I ended up with a pair of not-so-great parents, but at least they didn't beat me."

"They did in other ways." Cullen's warm breath caressed her neck. "I can't believe I'm saying this, but it's good they're out of your life. Neither deserves a daughter like you. "

And she didn't deserve Cullen. Because he needed someone who knew how to make relationships work. She didn't.

Tears stung. Sarah blinked them away.

"With your parents deserting you, how did you end up going to college and getting a PhD?"

"Being emancipated meant I didn't need my parents' income information for financial aid. I spent the first two years at a community college before transferring to a university. I paid using a combination of scholarships, grants, loans, and working multiple jobs at a time."

"I'm so proud of you." He kept holding her, and she let herself savor the closeness. "What you did, how hard you must have worked, shows you're not destined to repeat what your rotten parents did. You have a wonderful career. You can also have what they've never had—a good, solid relationship. One that lasts."

"Maybe I can do better than my parents." But no relationship lasted. She would end up alone and brokenhearted. The way she always had. "But I've learned my lesson. I can't jump into something…"

"That something is our marriage."

"You know what I mean."

"I do," he admitted. "But here's the deal. We don't have to jump into anything. We did that the first time around. It didn't work. There's nothing to stop us from going slower this second time."

A vise tightened around her heart. "I'm not going to be here much longer. We don't live in the same state."

"Long distance can't be any worse than being apart."

A flutter of hope emerged. "I suppose that's true."

"It is true. But don't decide right now," he said to her relief. "Think about it. Think about what it'll take to turn your 'I can't' into an 'I want to.' Will you do that for me? For us?"

Affection for Cullen deepened. He might have been a stranger when they got married, but she'd picked a great guy even if he had a few faults. "Yes, I will."

He squeezed her shoulder. "Now get some sleep."

She wanted him next to her all night. "Will you stay,

please?"

"You're going to have to kick me out. Though I can't promise you I won't sneak under the covers if it gets colder."

"You can get under them now."

"Let's not test my self-control too much." He kissed her forehead. "Sweet dreams, Lavagirl."

Sheltered in his arms, Sarah had a feeling she would have very sweet dreams. Maybe a couple of hot ones, too, starring the handsome and incredibly fit Dr. Gray. She hoped she woke up knowing the answer to his question.

What *would* it take to turn her "I can't" to "I want to"?

Chapter Twenty

The following morning, Cullen put away the dishes while Sarah studied the newest data from Mount Baker. Everything she'd told him last night tumbled around in his head. He couldn't believe they'd been married and knew so little about each other.

I've never seen or experienced a successful relationship.

He ached for her. But he needed to know about her past if they wanted their marriage to work. Sarah needed help to overcome the damage inflicted by her parents and ex-fiancé. It would take time to erase a lifetime of negative images, neglect, and verbal abuse. Therapy, together the way his family had done and also individually, would be a good start. Working through the past would help her move forward so they could work things out between them. If she wanted to work things out...

All he could do now was wait and hope.

The next two days passed quickly. Too quickly for Sarah. She had no idea what to say to Cullen. Fortunately, he'd been working at the hospital and on a ready team, so she could avoid the confrontation. But she couldn't put off the discussion much longer.

Rays of morning sunlight streamed in the kitchen window. Sarah made herself a cup of chamomile tea. Cullen sat at the kitchen table reading the paper. Today was the first of three days off for him. He'd wanted the break. She, however, had mixed feelings.

She tossed the tea bag in the garbage. "Want something to drink?"

"No, thanks. But I'll take another blueberry muffin. Then maybe we could talk."

She picked up a muffin, but nerves made her almost drop it. If Christmas magic did exist, in June or December or whenever, she wished it could come to the rescue now.

He glanced over the paper at her. "Sean invited us to a BBQ tomorrow night. Everyone will be there. I went ahead and told him we'd attend."

She hoped people wouldn't want to talk about her and Cullen. But given the phone calls after the dinner at the Willinghams' house, the chances of that were slim to none.

Her cell phone beeped with a text message.

"Must be Tucker," she said. "He's early this morning."

"If he wants you at work, tell him you're still recovering."

"I'm nearly self-sufficient now."

He studied her. "You ready to go to Bellingham?"

"No."

With a little smirk, he continued reading the paper.

Sarah's cell phone rang. Tucker's ringtone. That was odd, considering the text was most likely from him.

She sat in the recliner, picked up her phone, and saw *Steam Blast* on the screen. Her heart slammed against her chest. Forcing herself to breathe, she hit the answer button. "What's happening up there?"

Sarah's white-knuckled grip on the phone, her stiff posture, and the rise in her voice told Cullen all he needed to know. It was time for her to go. A weight pressed against his chest, right over his heart.

She disconnected the call.

He took a deep breath. "Tucker wants you at the institute."

"Another steam burst occurred this morning." She gathered her papers, hurriedly shoving them into her laptop bag. "Tucker needs me there. Now."

No. The word positioned itself on the tip of Cullen's

tongue, ready to spring out into the world. Sarah couldn't return to Bellingham. She wasn't healed enough. Not exactly true, but he would do or say whatever he had to in order to make her stay. He wasn't ready to let her go. If she went away, she might not come back. Especially with things so up in the air between them. "Now?"

"Tucker would have preferred having me there yesterday, but since we don't have a time machine handy..."

Cullen's cell phone vibrated. He glanced at the screen.

A rescue-mission callout. "I don't believe this."

She stopped her flurry of activity. "What?"

"Missing climbers."

Someone needed help on the mountain, but Sarah needed help here. Priorities waged battle against loyalty. He had a duty—two actually. The physician and mountain rescuer wanted to be part of the mission, to help whoever was in need. The husband wanted to be with his wife because he might not have much time left with her.

Cullen stood. "The unit's gathering at Timberline Lodge, but I can skip this one and drive you to Bellingham."

"You're needed on the rescue."

He could be. "I don't know the mission specifics. It might not be anything. I've missed missions when I was in the middle of a shift and couldn't get someone to cover for me. They'll have plenty of rescuers."

"You're the only doctor."

His throat thickened. "I'm driving you."

Neither moved or spoke. Stalemate.

"How long will your mission take?" she asked finally.

"I don't know."

She wrapped her fingers around her laptop. "What if I wait until you're finished? I need to pack my things. I can analyze data until you get home."

His heart swelled with relief, gratitude, and affection. "That would be wonderful. I'll be back as soon as I can."

"Don't rush on my account." Concern clouded her features. "Please be careful."

He wanted to wipe her worry away, wanted to take her in his arms and hold her close, wanted to tell her how much her waiting meant to him. Instead, he kissed her lightly on the lips, forcing himself not to take the kiss deeper. But he'd make up for it...later. "Always. We don't take needless risks up there."

The tip of her tongue darted out and moistened her lips. "I'm holding you to that."

Cullen wanted to taste her all over. *No time now.* "Please do."

His gear was packed due to an upcoming ready team, but he double-checked the equipment. He filled his water bottle. "I'll have someone check on you."

"Thanks, but there's no need. I've been through this when you were with the rescue group in Seattle. I'll be fine. As long as I know..."

"Know what?"

Sarah's tender smile washed over him. "That you're safe."

Her concern tugged at his heart. Cullen didn't want to leave her. He didn't want her to leave him. "Rescuer safety is priority number one. Our mission plans are built around that."

"I know." Sarah didn't sound convinced.

He didn't want her to worry about him. "If you don't want me to go—"

"Go." She cut him off. "I'm being…silly."

He ran his index finger along her jawline. "You're cute when you're silly."

She stuck her tongue out at him.

Cullen laughed. If only it could always be like this between them. But she was needed in Bellingham. For now. Maybe not for long. Her postdoc position wouldn't last forever. He kissed her forehead. "Pack your things. I'll be home before you know it."

When he returned, he would tell her that she always had a place here with him. That he hoped she would come back soon. That he hoped she would want to stay. Because he wanted her with him. He prayed she felt the same way.

At two o'clock, snow fell from the darkening sky. Sarah

couldn't believe another storm was hitting in June. Especially with three climbers missing and rescue teams searching for them.

More data downloaded from MBVI's server. Tucker wasn't happy she was still in Hood Hamlet, but she was doing what she could from here.

She pressed her cheek against the window. The cold stung her skin, but she kept her face there. Cullen had to be freezing wherever he was. Wet, too. She prayed he was okay.

The doorbell rang.

Sarah jumped. Maybe Cullen had finished with the mission. She hurried to open the door.

A woman in her forties with short curly hair stood on the front porch. "I'm looking for Sarah Purcell."

Brrr. Goose bumps covered Sarah's skin. "That's me."

"I have a delivery from this company." The woman pointed to the name Haskell, Thayer, and Henry printed on a large white envelope and then handed it to Sarah. "Please sign this acceptance of service acknowledging you received the papers."

Sarah tucked the envelope under her arm. She scribbled her signature with her left hand.

The woman thanked her before returning to her car.

Sarah went into the cabin, as if moving in slow motion. Her fingers gripped the envelope. She didn't need to open the flap to know what was inside. Well, she was ninety-nine percent certain.

I knew you were busy, so once I established residency in Oregon, I got things started there.

They know I filed for divorce.

Divorce papers. Her stomach roiled. Sarah thought she might be sick. Okay, he'd filed before her accident, but knowing that still hurt. Holding them now…

Sarah plodded into the kitchen. Dropped the unopened envelope on the breakfast bar. She had too much to worry about with him on the mountain in a storm and the second steam blast on Mount Baker.

Hours passed. Sarah studied the data and spoke with Tucker over Skype. But what she wanted was to hear from Cullen. A phone call. A text.

The doorbell rang.

She was almost afraid to answer the door again, but she did. The wind whipped. Snow fell in a solid sheet of white. Carly, Zoe, and Christian Welton stood on the porch, bundled up in parkas and hats.

Sarah invited them in. She assumed Cullen had asked his friends to check on her. She was glad he'd done that even though she'd told him not to. She needed the company. "I can't believe you three ventured out in this kind of weather."

"We wanted to see how you were doing." Zoe removed her hat, scarf, coat, and mittens, and then hung them on the hat tree. "We also have some news."

Sarah forced herself not to hold her breath. "Good news, I hope."

Carly hung her coat. "Rescue Team Four found the

missing climbers and brought them down."

Relief flowed through Sarah, loosening her tense muscles. "That's wonderful. Everyone will be home soon."

Forget about the divorce papers. Sarah wiggled her toes with anticipation. She wanted to see Cullen.

"Almost everyone," Christian said. "Teams Two and Three are stuck on the mountain. They'll be down once there's a break in the weather."

"Is Cullen on one of those teams?" she asked.

Carly nodded. "Sean, Jake, Bill, Tim, and Cullen are hunkering down in a snow cave. They're fine, but the conditions are bad up there."

The hair on Sarah's arms stood on end. That didn't sound good.

"The guys made the smart decision, given the conditions," Christian said. "Leanne and the rest of Team Three reached the Palmer lift station before the whiteout made continuing their descent too dangerous. They'll stay there tonight."

Worried, Sarah chewed on her lower lip.

"Everyone is fine," Carly reiterated. "But staying put will keep them safe tonight."

Sarah had slept in a snow cave as part of an alpine mountaineering course she'd taken. A snow cave would protect the team from the elements. That was crucial in this kind of weather. But she would rather have Cullen home.

Zoe raised a paper sack. "We brought dinner."

"No reason to sit alone when we're all in the same boat," Christian explained.

Carly nodded. "We stopped by Tim's place, but Rita and Wyatt are at her parents' house in Portland. The other guys on Rescue Three live down the mountain."

Sarah appreciated their thoughtfulness. Food was the last thing on her mind, but she needed to eat. To keep up her strength. She wanted to be strong for Cullen. "Thanks. This is so nice of you."

Carly touched Sarah's arm. "It's good for all of us."

"Where's Nicole?" Sarah asked.

"With Hannah and Garrett," Carly said. "Jake and I were supposed to have a date night."

"Skip the barbecue tomorrow night and go on your date instead," Zoe suggested.

Carly hugged Zoe. "Thanks, but we'll go out another night."

As they prepared dinner, Sarah realized in the short time she'd been in Hood Hamlet, she'd made good friends. Something she hadn't had before. Some of that was due to her job, but part—a big part—was the change in her. She didn't let people get close. In Hood Hamlet, that hadn't stopped them from butting their noses into her life. Having them do that wasn't such a bad thing.

Zoe set the table. "I'm happy we're together tonight. When I'm at the base volunteering, I'm not so impatient. But I hate waiting."

"Me, too." Sarah would give anything to touch Cullen right now. "I wish the snow would stop."

"Rescuer safety is the priority when they're on a mission," Zoe explained. "Sean tells me that over and over again."

Carly nodded. "Jake, too."

Christian prepared chicken marsala. "Add Leanne to the list."

Sarah sighed. "Cullen said the same thing to me."

Zoe put napkins at each of the four place settings. "What they don't understand is no matter what the conditions are, when the love of your life is up on the mountain, all you can do is worry."

Sarah nodded in agreement.

Wait a minute.

The love of her life?

Cullen?

Truth scorched like the hot lava from Kilauea in Hawaii.

Oh, no. She wasn't falling for Cullen. She'd fallen.

She loved him. Truly loved him. With her heart, body, and soul.

How had she let that happen?

Sarah folded her left arm over her stomach.

Zoe rushed to Sarah's side. "You're so pale. Sit."

She sat.

Christian knelt, taking her pulse. "Does anything hurt?"

"No." Her voice cracked.

Carly touched Sarah's forehead with the back of her hand. "You don't feel warm."

"I'm not sick." Not unless they counted being lovesick. "Give me a minute. I'm lightheaded."

A worried glance passed between Carly and Christian. His forehead wrinkled. "With your injuries, you probably can't put your head between your legs, but bend over a little if you can."

Sarah did. She hated making her friends worry when the problem wasn't her injuries. But what could she say? That she'd realized she loved her husband? Loved him to the point nothing else mattered?

"Feel better?" Carly asked.

"Yes."

Physically, Sarah did. But emotionally…

This was the worst thing ever. Loving Cullen gave him complete power over her, to hurt her when he no longer wanted her. And he wouldn't want her to be with him forever.

How could he?

No one else had.

Building a volcano and playing with a toddler didn't mean she would be a good mother. She didn't know anything about being a mom, let alone being a decent one. Not to mention being Cullen's wife. She could try, but she would end up failing as before. And that would hurt them both.

Zoe handed her a glass of water. "Take a sip."

Sarah raised her head and drank.

Christian studied her face. "Your color's returning."

"I'm feeling better," she said.

But her heart was breaking. Thank goodness her things were packed. If Cullen asked her to stay, she wouldn't be able to leave him. That would end up a disaster. The longer she remained with him, the more they'd hurt when the relationship ended. She couldn't do that to Cullen again. She wouldn't do that to him.

Or herself.

She had to end things now. No going back. No second chance. No matter how tempted she might be.

Sarah glanced at the envelope containing the divorce papers. She didn't know whether they needed to be signed or what. But once she figured it out, she could leave. Cullen hadn't tried to win her back before. He wouldn't this time.

Her heart cried out at the thought.

No, she wouldn't let emotion overwhelm her.

This was for the best. Sarah wasn't strong enough to survive being dumped again. She wasn't sure she was strong enough to leave him on her own. She would have to take off before he got home.

Sarah drank the rest of her water. "I'm okay now. Really."

The relief on her three friends' faces coated her mouth with guilt. But this was for the...best. She would be gone before Cullen returned.

Coward, a voice mocked.

Not a coward. Smart. Proactive. This was the best way—the only way—to keep her heart safe.

Chapter Twenty-One

Cullen supposed there were worse places he could be than a snow cave in the middle of a blizzard on Mount Hood with four of his closest friends. Someday he might laugh about this but not tonight.

At least they were safe, and so were the missing climbers. Three lives had been saved. No sense risking theirs. As soon as the weather cleared, they would head down. Until then, they would make the best of the situation.

He sipped from his water bottle—snow he'd melted using his lightweight portable gas stove. A good thing to have on this chilly night, but he'd rather be cuddling with Sarah.

Cullen missed her. He would miss her more when she left Hood Hamlet.

But he understood. Mount Baker was blowing off steam. He didn't blame her for wanting to be at the institute.

"Whose bright idea was it to sleep out here?" Hughes asked.

"Paulson's," Porter, Moreno, and Cullen said at the same time.

"Just a suggestion." Paulson scooted deeper inside his sleeping bag. "I didn't think anyone would take me seriously."

"You know Doc," Porter teased. "He's always serious."

Cullen stuck his water bottle inside his sleeping bag to keep it from freezing. "Someone needs to be serious around you clowns."

Hughes grinned. "I'm sure Doc's all fun and games when he's with Sarah."

"We may be different, but she keeps me smiling." Cullen would give anything to feel her snuggled up against him. His temperature rose a degree, maybe two. That might work to his advantage here.

"Being opposites is good." Moreno held his water bottle with his gloved hands. "Rita can't stand anything I like to do except hike, and that's only when the weather's sunny and warm. But she's amazing. I couldn't imagine being married to anyone else."

"Rough life having one gourmet meal after another cooked for you." Hughes laughed. "Unlike me with a gorgeous wife who can't boil water without the fire department showing up."

"It's amazing Moreno isn't pushing three hundred pounds," Paulson teased.

Moreno smirked. "I burn off the calories other ways."

"Yeah, chasing little Wyatt," Hughes joked.

"That's right." Porter laughed. "Kids make those long, lazy mornings spent in bed a thing of the past."

Moreno unwrapped a granola bar. "Unless the kids are with you."

Porter nodded. "I can't wait to see my girls. I'd love one of Carly's cookies right now."

"She'll have a plateful at the base when we get down," Hughes said.

Moreno nodded. "And Zoe will be there with piping-hot cups of coffee."

A faraway expression filled Hughes's face. He tightened the cord on his jacket's hood. "Too bad she can't deliver up here."

Paulson scrunched his face as if he'd swallowed something sour. "Marriage has turned you all into a bunch of saps. Well, except Doc. He's the same as always."

Cullen wasn't sure that was a compliment. He wiggled his fingers to keep them warm.

"Nah." Hughes shook his head. "Doc smiles more now."

"I actually heard him laugh," Porter teased.

"Very funny, guys," Cullen said.

Things might be up in the air between him and Sarah, but for all their troubles, he couldn't deny he was a better man for knowing her. She brought spontaneity to his life.

Tried to make him see what was important, that there was more to living than making plans. Just because he lost control didn't mean he was going to fall over the edge as Blaine had. He wouldn't with Sarah as his anchor.

Even though he was stuck up here, she kept his thoughts focused. She was good for him. Not dangerous.

Sarah had soothed his fears about Paulson. She'd been the reason Cullen had talked about his brother and family when that was the last thing he wanted to do.

Being open was Cullen's biggest fear, not being reckless. The people he was closest with, people like Sarah and Blaine, could hurt Cullen the most and send his emotions out of control. But this second time with Sarah, being open with her had made him stronger, not weaker. The same with Blaine's memory.

But Cullen hadn't realized that until now. Would acknowledging the truth be enough to keep Sarah from leaving? He didn't know, nor did he care. But he knew one thing. Love was worth the risk.

When everyone had gone home after dinner, Sarah picked up the white envelope. With a trembling hand, she removed the papers—a dissolution of marriage petition. She read each sheet. Neither had assets the other wanted to claim, so the wording was cut and dried. If she agreed with the petition, she didn't have to respond. The paperwork would go before a judge, and their marriage would be over.

With a blue pen in her left hand, she set the tip against another piece of paper. Tears fell. She wiped them away. Her heart didn't want her to write this note, but she'd learned long ago she couldn't trust her heart.

Ignoring the pain in her chest, Sarah refocused. Her heart thudded like a bass drum. The steady beat brought to mind a post-battle scene where those who had survived the melee gathered the bodies of dead soldiers. She pushed the graphic image from her mind.

This wasn't war. More like a surrender, a quiet one without any fanfare.

With a shaky hand, she wrote what needed to be said and scribbled her signature at the end.

There.

She dropped the pen.

It was done. Over.

She inhaled, thinking she would feel better. Instead, she felt worse.

For the best.

She'd better get busy. The shuttle would arrive soon to take her to the airport.

Sarah placed the divorce papers in the white envelope, set them on the breakfast bar, and then placed the note on top.

Last night, she'd pulled her wedding ring out of the zippered pocket in her toiletry kit and stuck the gold band on her finger. She'd wanted to wear it one last time. For old times' sake…

Sarah slowly removed the ring that slipped off her finger as easily as it had gone on. She placed the band on top of the note. And her heart wept.

Chapter Twenty-Two

*H*ome.

Anticipation pulsed through Cullen's veins. He dumped his backpack in the garage. He would unpack his gear later. All he wanted was to see Sarah.

He entered the house. "Sarah."

She didn't answer.

That was odd, but a sense of foreboding was strong. She wasn't there.

Shoulders hunched, Cullen went into the living room. He understood Sarah's need to go to Bellingham, to her job at the institute. Reporters had been abuzz with news of additional steam blasts and earthquakes. Granted, he'd been stuck in a snow cave overnight, but to take off without so much as a goodbye...

A white envelope on the breakfast bar caught his attention.

A two-ton weight pressed down on him. He trudged to the kitchen, feeling as if he were wading through quicksand. A note and her gold wedding band sat on top of the envelope. With unsteady hands, he unfolded the piece of paper.

Dear Cullen,

I appreciate all you've done for me these past weeks. Hood Hamlet has been the perfect place to recover. Thank you for opening your home to me and introducing me to your friends.

I know you wanted to drive me home to Bellingham, but after being stuck overnight in a snow cave, the last thing you need is to be stuck in a car making the long drive there and back.

The dissolution of marriage petition was served yesterday. I do still want a divorce. I agree with everything in the paperwork, and I will not be filing a response. Very soon, there will be nothing stopping you from getting your life on track.

I wish you the best. Heaven knows you deserve better than someone like me. I'm sure you'll find her, and she'll be exactly what you want in a wife.

Sarah

No! Cullen crumpled the page into a tight ball. Wanting to scream, shout, or hit something, he threw the note. The paper bounced off the wall and fell to the floor.

Familiar anger and resentment exploded. Hands shaking, Cullen picked up her wedding ring. He ran his fingers around the smooth gold band. Sarah hadn't seemed the sentimental type, yet she'd kept hers. As he'd kept his. He set the ring on the bar.

The silence and emptiness of the cabin matched his

desolation.

Was this how Sarah had felt when she'd arrived home from doing research on Mount Baker and discovered he'd moved out while she was away? Cullen didn't want to know the answer. She didn't deserve any sympathy.

Couldn't Sarah see they had something special? Why would she leave this way?

He stiffened.

Leave like he had when she'd brought up a divorce.

Cullen retrieved the wadded-up note, smoothed the wrinkles from the page, and reread it. Again and again. And then something clicked.

Sarah wasn't leaving him for something better. She wanted him to find something—*someone*—better than her. This wasn't about him or them, but her. For some reason, she didn't think she was good enough.

Just like the last time. But he'd been too hurt, too full of pride, to realize it.

Snippets of conversations rushed to the surface.

I've never felt so inadequate in my life.

I wasn't anything special. I would have held him back. I don't blame him for not wanting to marry me.

They didn't care about me. They never wanted me around. After the divorce, they shuttled me back and forth.

All the pieces had been there, one after another, but Cullen hadn't put them together. Until now.

He needed to go after Sarah and show her how special she was, how much he needed her. Something her mom and dad had never done, or her idiotic fiancé, or…

Him.

His chest tightened, squeezing the air out of his lungs. He'd let Sarah down a year ago. No, he'd let her down from the time they'd returned to Seattle after she'd rocked his neat and tidy little world. He'd kept parts of his life separate from her. He'd been afraid of losing control, of following in Blaine's footsteps into addiction by becoming obsessed with something or someone that would be bad for him. Cullen had held on tight to what he could and kept her out.

What had the family counselor called it?

Compartmentalizing.

He'd gone further than that. He'd built walls, remained silent, and run away.

When Sarah had mentioned divorce, he'd jumped at the chance to make a clean break and then retreated like a turtle into its shell to lick his wounds. What he'd failed to see was how good Sarah was for him.

So good.

He wasn't going to make the same mistake again. He would go to Bellingham and convince her they belonged together. Do whatever it took. Fight for her if he had to.

At this point, he had nothing to lose except…everything.

Sitting at her desk at MBVI, Sarah studied the

seismographic signals. Around her, the atmosphere crackled with energy, phones rang at a frenetic rate, and people carried equipment out of the building in order to set up additional monitoring stations a safe distance away from the volcano.

Seismic activity from inside Mount Baker's crater had quadrupled in frequency since the steam blast. Whatever was going on could fizzle out, but until that happened, she had work to do. Anticipation over the possibilities ahead buzzed through her, but something kept her feet firmly planted on the ground.

Not something.

Someone.

Cullen.

She leaned forward in her chair, not wanting thoughts of him to swamp her.

The new and exciting seismic signals should be her only concern, but Sarah kept thinking about Hood Hamlet. She missed the town, the people, Cullen. She'd taken off with so many unknowns.

Had he and his rescue team made it off the mountain safely? Had he arrived home and read her note? Did he hate her?

Sarah rubbed her tired eyes before refocusing on the data.

Tucker placed a steaming cup of coffee and a chocolate bar on the left side of her desk. "You've been working nonstop."

The candy reminded her of the chocolate tasting

with Cullen and his hot kiss. He would never be kissing her again.

A knife twisted inside her.

Maybe caffeine would help her concentrate. She took a sip of coffee. "That's why you hired me."

"I hired you because you're qualified and smart." Tucker sat on the edge of her desk. Her boss was in his late thirties, wearing jeans and a T-shirt. He looked more like a rugged cowboy than a nerdy, calculator-toting scientist. "You're still recovering. Don't overdo it."

"There's data to review."

"And more coming," he admitted. "I wanted you here, but I don't want you to overdo it and end up slowing your recovery. You don't have to get through everything right now. Think of it as job security."

She straightened. "My funding runs out soon."

"I always have an ace or two up my sleeve. And I have a feeling I'm going to need you around." Tucker had built MBVI from the ground up with lots of sweat, begging, and a generous donation from a mysterious anonymous benefactor. He glanced in the direction of Mount Baker. "I'm just relieved you're here. I half expected to receive a call from the Cascades Volcano Observatory asking for a reference so they could hire you."

She flinched. "Why would you think that?"

"Cullen. He was so worried about you at the hospital."

Memories stirred beneath her breastbone. Of him, of

her, of them. No, she couldn't go there. "He's a doctor. *Concerned* is his middle name."

"He was more than concerned."

How would Tucker know anything about that? "It doesn't matter. The divorce petition has been filed. I'm not challenging anything. Our marriage is over."

"I'm sorry for you both, but that's one less thing to take you away from here." Tucker stood. "One more hour maximum. Absolutely no more than that or I'll kick you out myself. Feel free to leave earlier, but don't make any detours. I want you to go home and sleep."

Her muscles tightened. Steam was still rising from the crater. "I'll sleep when Baker sleeps."

"Now that you're back, I can't afford to lose you."

Sarah straightened, but what her boss said didn't fill the emptiness inside her. Once she'd found total fulfillment in her work. Now she realized she'd been using her job to mask the loneliness, the hurt, and the ache left by the failure of her marriage. The loss of Cullen.

"We have to figure out when something else might happen up there," Tucker continued. "You need to be in top form. Rested. Ready for anything. Got it?"

Sarah knew that tone. No worries. She could work remotely from her apartment. "Got it."

"And no working from home, either."

She sighed. "Yes, sir."

Thirty minutes later, her forehead throbbed. Eyestrain, tiredness, or…a broken heart? Most likely a combination of all three. She massaged her temples.

Maybe Tucker was right about going home. After she closed her laptop, she slid it into her bag. She said goodbye to her coworkers before exiting the institute.

Outside, she glanced up at Mount Baker. The plume of steam contrasted against the blue sky. A gray, overcast day would have matched her mood and the volcano's much better.

"Sarah."

The sound of Cullen's voice sent chills through her. He was leaning against the building. The sight of him in a pair of faded jeans and a short-sleeved shirt made her mouth go dry. She had to be way more tired than she realized if she was imagining him here.

Sarah blinked. Still there. She wasn't hallucinating. She pinched herself. Not dreaming, either.

"Why are you here?" she asked.

He straightened. "You forgot something."

No way. Sarah had been extra careful when she packed, to make sure she had everything that belonged to her. "What did I forget?"

Cullen raised his chin slightly, his jaw tight. "Me."

Her mouth gaped. The air whooshed from her lungs. She couldn't breathe.

He moved toward her slowly, as if each step were planned, calculated, with intent and purpose. "You're busy with important work, so I brought me to you."

She tried to speak but couldn't.

He reached forward and ran his hand along her cheek.

267

Sarah fought the urge to sink into his touch. She had to be strong. For both their sakes.

His gaze ran the length of her. "You have a headache."

How did he know that? Her brain whirled with questions, fatigue, and a heavy dose of confusion. "I don't understand why you're here."

Cullen pulled something from behind his back. It must have been tucked in the waistband of his jeans. A white envelope. The divorce papers. "You left these for me."

Her heart thudded with dread. "We'll be divorced soon."

Holding the envelope out in front of him, he tore the top portion.

She reached forward to stop him. "What are you doing?"

"What I should have done a year ago to put an end to any talk of a divorce." He ripped the envelope in half. "Worst money I ever spent."

She stared, stunned. "It doesn't matter. The petition has been filed."

"I told my attorney to halt the proceeding."

Her mouth dropped. She closed it. "We'll have to start over."

"That's all I want. For us to start over."

Disbelief and hope warred inside her.

"I don't want a divorce, Sarah. I've never wanted one, but I was too hurt to realize it. I love you. Only you."

"Love is…"

"The only thing that matters." He took her left hand. "I haven't been the best husband. After what happened to Blaine, I was afraid to lose control and wind up like him. You overwhelmed me from the moment we met. It was great at first. I felt whole again, but I got scared. Thought I was too obsessed and becoming addicted to you. I clung to control where I could. Ran away when I couldn't. Didn't open myself up. Compartmentalized everything. My work. My emotions. Our marriage. You. That wasn't right. Or fair. No wonder you wanted to leave. You deserved better from me. I'm finally ready to give it to you. If you want it. Want me."

A gush of warmth flowed through Sarah's veins. She fought the urge to soak up the love he was offering. "Oh, I appreciate this. You'll never know how much. But I've seen what happened with my parents and stepparents. Even if we wanted to make it work, marriages don't last."

He squeezed her hand. "I know you've seen marriages fail. You've lived through breakups way too many times. But the divorce rate isn't one hundred percent. Some marriages *do* last. Ours can if we're willing to work on it. Fight for it. I know you're a fighter. So am I."

She wanted to believe, but something—fear, maybe—held her back. "Even if we fought for it, I don't know how to be a good wife like Hannah, Carly, and Zoe. You need someone who's worthy of you. Perfect for you. That isn't me."

"You might not think you're the perfect wife, but you're the perfect wife for me." Cullen pressed her hand against his mouth. Kissed it. "I was afraid of losing myself in you. The way Blaine lost himself in drugs. What I failed to see is how good you are for me. You're the best thing that's ever happened to me. You fill me up and set me free. You make me stronger. Nothing wrong with that at all."

Her heart sighed. Still more protests rose to her lips. "But—"

"I don't care that you'd rather be covered in mud or ash than wear something frilly. Or that you prefer cooking on a glacier than in a gourmet kitchen. I love that you're willing to run toward an erupting volcano if it means getting the data you need even while everyone else is running away. That's the woman I love, the woman I married, the woman I want to grow old with."

Tears stung. Feelings of inadequacy shot arrows through her. She sniffled. "But you deserve better."

"You do, too. I'm far from the perfect man or husband. I tend to see things my way. Sometimes, I'm too serious."

"Sometimes?"

He grinned. "A lot of times. I don't have a clue how to show how I'm feeling."

Love for this man bubbled in her soul. "You're doing a good job right now."

"It isn't easy," he admitted. "But you're worth it. We both have a lot to learn and work to do. We have to keep talking and not close ourselves off again. Therapy would do us both good. A lot of things can go wrong, but we can make this work. I have no doubt. But we'll never know unless we're willing to take a chance. I am. If you are, I trust you'll stick it out even if things get a little rough. Up for it?"

Hope was starting to win. "I would love to believe our life, our future, could be spent together, not apart."

He kissed her on the lips. "Believe it. Stay my wife."

If ever she had a chance at a forever kind of love, she wanted it with Cullen. His coming for her proved he knew her, understood her, sometimes better than she knew herself. But fear kept whispering all the things that could go wrong. She was afraid of being disappointed, of being abandoned. But fear wasn't a good enough reason for walking away from something that had the potential to be so wonderful.

"Yes." Sarah was afraid, but willing, oh so willing. She kissed him, a kiss full of her hopes and dreams for the two of them. "I love you. I want to make this work more than anything, but I'm terrified. I'm so scared about how things could go wrong again."

"I'm afraid, too, but it'll be okay because we're together." His warm breath caressed her skin. He hugged her. "We are going to make this work. We'll make it through whatever comes up."

Hope overflowed from her heart. "So what happens now?"

He removed two gold bands from his pocket. He slid

hers on her ring finger. "Your turn."

She placed the other on his finger.

"You'll need to show me where we live," he said. "Then I need to get my résumé together so I can drop a copy off at the hospital."

She stared at him in disbelief. "What?"

"I love living in Hood Hamlet, but I love you more. I want to be where you are, whether it's here by Mount Baker or wherever you end up. Most places need doctors. And we can always move to Hood Hamlet when the time is right."

"I want to live there. It's the perfect place to raise a family."

"I agree. But until we're ready for that, let's play it by ear and see what happens. Plans can be so overrated."

Her heart swelled with love and respect for her husband. "You are amazing, Dr. Gray."

"You're not so bad yourself, Lavagirl."

As Cullen kissed her, the ground trembled. Another earthquake from Mount Baker.

Contentment and joy flowed through Sarah. She didn't need the sparkling castles with gleaming turrets she'd read about as a child. A steam-blasting volcano in the northern Cascades was the perfect backdrop for the beginning of her and Cullen's fairy tale and true love's kiss.

Epilogue

As Sarah stared out the passenger window of Cullen's truck, the colorful decorations on Main Street filled her with holiday cheer. The music inside the cab matched the scenery perfectly. Storefront windows glowed with lights and displays. Wreaths hung on doors. Even the old-fashioned lampposts had been decked out with lights and ribbons. December in Hood Hamlet was more beautiful than she could have imagined. "So where's this Christmas magic everyone talks about?"

"It's not like pixie dust or anything you can see, but Christmas magic is all around." Cullen motioned to the garland with a wreath hanging from the center that was strung over the street every fifteen feet. To a snowman with an *Experience the Magic* sign greeting visitors just off the edge of the wooden sidewalk. To a charming Nativity scene set up in front of a church. "Here in town and everywhere on the mountain."

Listening to her husband talk about something that

couldn't be seen or touched filled her with joy. He'd opened himself up to so much, including her.

She and Cullen were working on their marriage and themselves. Couples counseling wasn't easy, but there'd been more steps forward than back. Both were committed to their relationship. They needed to keep talking and not take anything, especially each other, for granted. "I'll keep my eyes and ears open."

He shot her a sideward glance. "Are you starting to believe?"

"I like the idea of it. A part of me wants to believe." Magic fell into the realm of Santa Claus and the tooth fairy, but given how far they'd come as a couple over the past few months, she wasn't about to make any hasty conclusions. "So I'm open to the possibility."

"Fair enough." He sounded pleased, which made her happy. "We'll find evidence while we're here to convince you."

"You sound confident."

He tapped his thumb to the Christmas song playing on the radio. "I am."

They were in town until December twenty-sixth. He'd wanted her to experience a Hood Hamlet Christmas. Somehow, they'd both managed the time off. Her postdoc had finished, but Tucker had found funds to keep her on staff. Cullen worked in a nearby emergency department and volunteered with the local mountain rescue unit.

As they drove past the general store, Bill Paulson

waved from the sidewalk. She returned the gesture.

A happy sigh welled up inside Sarah. "It's good to be in Hood Hamlet."

Cullen grinned. "We were just here for Thanksgiving."

The meal had defined her new family—one of choice, not blood. "I know, but…"

"This is home."

She nodded, knowing he understood. Hood Hamlet might not be where they physically lived at the moment, but this was where they would settle eventually. Since moving to Bellingham in June, friends from here had visited them. She and Cullen had returned to town when they could, a necessity with the many pre-wedding festivities for Leanne and Christian.

Sarah tapped her toes against the floorboard. "I can't believe tomorrow is the big day. I can't wait to hear Leanne and Christian exchange vows."

"Me, either." Cullen reached across and squeezed her hand, one of his fingers brushing her gold wedding band. He'd offered to buy her a diamond ring—whatever she wanted—but what they had was perfect. She didn't need more.

Only him.

The vows she and Cullen had exchanged inside that Las Vegas chapel held more meaning to them after everything they'd been through. Maybe one day, they'd renew their vows in front of their friends, but that wasn't necessary now. Watching the video of their ceremony—

the two of them giddy with adoration for the other—was enough. She didn't want to change their history, only learn from it so they didn't make the same mistakes in the future.

As Cullen sang along to a new Christmas carol playing, Sarah studied his profile. Handsome, yes, but nothing was more beautiful than her husband's heart.

Warmth flowed through her. "I love you."

"I love you, too." He raised her arm and kissed her hand. "I have a surprise for you, Lavagirl."

His playful tone filled her with anticipation. "What, Dr. Gray?"

He shook his head. "Patience, my love."

Were they doing another chocolate tasting? Or meeting their friends at the brewpub? Each time she had an idea, another popped into her mind.

"Trying to figure it out?" he asked.

She nodded.

He laughed, a sound she never tired of hearing. "You only have to wait a few more minutes."

"I'm not sure I can last that long." Who was she kidding? She'd wait for this man forever.

Cullen took a right onto a street she didn't recognize. Homes were tucked off the road in between tall pines.

"Did you rent a new place for us to stay?" she asked.

Nodding, he pulled into the driveway of a newer two-story log cabin complete with lights hanging from the eaves and a front porch. "What do you think?"

"It's gorgeous." They'd been staying at the inn on

Main Street, but renting a house for the holidays made sense, even if the house was bigger than the two of them needed. "Christmas is the time for splurges."

"My feeling exactly." After he turned off the engine, he removed the key from the ignition.

She exited the truck.

Cullen was at her side, his fingers lacing with hers. "Let's take a tour of the house first."

"Sure."

Sarah followed him to the porch. Someone had cleared the path. A wreath with holly, pinecones, and a large red bow hung on the door. *Home Sweet Home* was written on the welcome mat. As if on cue, two deer ran across the front yard.

A touch of Christmas magic?

Happy to have this time together, Sarah leaned into Cullen. "I don't care what the inside is like. I love the cabin already. Thanks for finding it."

He kissed her forehead. "I wish I could take the credit, but Jake and Carly are the ones who suggested it. They know the owners."

Of course they did. Everyone in Hood Hamlet knew each other.

Cullen removed the key from the lock box and opened the door. Warmth flowed out, welcoming them to their home for the holidays.

Sarah took a step inside, but Cullen stopped her.

"What?" she asked.

"This." He picked her up.

She laughed. "What are you doing?"

"Carrying you over the threshold." His affectionate tone matched the love in his gaze. "Consider this a belated honeymoon."

"Oh." She cuddled against him. "I like that idea."

Even though each day since he'd joined her in Bellingham had felt like a honeymoon, despite their working to make their marriage stronger.

He brought her into the house, kicked the door closed, and kissed her on the lips.

She soaked up his taste and heat. "I could get used to this."

With a grin, he set her on the wide-plank hardwood floors. "I can never get enough of you, Lavagirl."

Knowing the feeling, Sarah winked. "Keep talking, Dr. Gray, and we'll never get our luggage out of the truck."

The cabin had an open-floor plan with beamed ceilings and interior designer touches that added character. A stone fireplace with a large wooden mantel was the focal point of the great room. Though a seven-foot artificial Christmas tree topped with a gold star was impossible to miss. White lights glowed. Icicles and snowflakes hung from the branches. Some were made of crystal and plastic. Others from paper and cardboard. She'd never considered a themed tree before, but the result was nothing but charming.

She took in the overstuffed furniture, the artwork, and the old-fashioned skis hanging on the wall. "The place is so homey."

He opened a pair of doors that she hadn't noticed. "There's even an office."

She tilted her head. "I hope you're not planning to work, because I'm not. I told Tucker not to disturb me during our Christmas vacation unless there's an eruption."

"No work." Cullen ran a finger along her jawline. "Just making sure you see everything."

She entered the kitchen with its sage-green cabinets, tiled backsplash, and white counters. Deep red and copper accents and accessories gave the décor a fresh feel. The table in the dining area appeared to be made of hickory, and the chairs had been painted the same sage color.

"I love it." She opened the stainless-steel refrigerator. A bottle of champagne was inside. The affection in her heart for her husband swelled. He'd thought of everything for their vacation—honeymoon. "We may have to make this place our home away from home."

"I was thinking the same thing." He pointed to another door. "That's a half bath."

This was so nice she could picture a family living here full time. "Let's see the second floor."

Side by side, they bounded up the stairs to view two smaller bedrooms, a laundry room, and a full bath. They only needed to see what was behind two double doors. "Is that the master bedroom?"

"Let's find out." Cullen opened the doors with a

flourish and then motioned her inside. "What do you think?"

A king-sized bed graced one wall with matching nightstands on either side of the mattress. A tall dresser sat against the wall to the left. There was a fireplace, along with an oversized chair and ottoman. In the bathroom, she glimpsed a double-headed shower, two sinks, and a separate toilet area. The layout was both practical and luxurious. "Wow."

"That's what I thought when I saw the pictures."

"I love it, but this feels more like a home than a vacation rental."

A beat passed. And another. "It could be both."

Could be? She stared at him. "What do you mean?"

"The owners used to live here full time. They've been renting out the house for the past year, but are planning to sell it in January."

Her pulse kicked up a notch.

"If we wanted to buy now and rent it out until we're ready to move back…" Cullen continued. "Jake says the property would be a good investment for the future. Bill, who owns rental houses, agrees."

She threw herself into Cullen's arms. "Who cares about the investment potential? This would be the perfect home for us."

"I agree." He kissed her as if to seal the deal. "We'll have a better idea if the house is right for us after our stay."

Sarah had a feeling they would know sooner than

that. "Have I told you how much I love you, Dr. Gray?"

"You may have mentioned it." He kissed her again. "And the feeling is mutual, Lavagirl."

She hugged him. "Thanks for making this Christmas so special."

He brushed his lips over her hair. "It's only the beginning."

Sarah couldn't wait for what came next.

Outside, snow fell. A large, intricate snowflake landed against the window as if hand-pressed against the glass.

Christmas magic is all around.

She had a feeling *it* was here with her and Cullen. And always would be.

Thank you for reading *His Second Chance*. I hope you enjoyed Sarah and Cullen's story. This is the fourth book in the Mountain Rescue Romance series. The other books feature Jake Porter, Sean Hughes, Leanne Thomas, and Bill Paulson.

Join my newsletter to receive a FREE story and hear about new releases, sales, freebies, and giveaways. Just go to melissamcclone.com/NLsignup.

I appreciate your help spreading the word. Tell a friend who loves sweet romance about this book and leave a review on your favorite book site. Reviews help readers find books!

Thanks so much!

About the Author

USA Today bestselling author Melissa McClone has written over forty-five sweet contemporary romance novels. She lives in the Pacific Northwest with her husband, three children, a spoiled Norwegian Elkhound, and cats who think they rule the house. They do!

If you'd like to find Melissa online, visit her at:

Website: www.melissamcclone.com
Email: melissa@melissamcclone.com
Page: facebook.com/melissamcclonebooks
Reader group: facebook.com/groups/mcclonetroopers

Other Books by Melissa Mcclone

Beach Brides & Indigo Bay Sweet Romance Series
Prequels to the Berry Lake Cupcake Posse series…
Jenny
Sweet Holiday Wishes
Sweet Beginnings
Sweet Do-Over
Sweet Yuletide
The Indigo Bay Sweet Romance Collection

The Billionaires of Silicon Forest
Who will be the last single man standing?
The Wife Finder
The Wish Maker
The Deal Breaker
The Gold Digger
The Kiss Catcher
The Game Changer

A Keeper Series
These men know what they want, and love isn't on their
list. But what happens when each meets a keeper?
The Groom
The Soccer Star
The Boss
The Husband
The Date
The Tycoon

Quinn Valley Ranch
Two books featuring siblings in a multi-author series...
Carter's Cowgirl
Summer Serenade
Quinn Valley Ranch Two Book Set

Her Royal Duty
Royal romances with
charming princes and dreamy castles...
The Reluctant Princess
The Not-So-Proper Princess
The Proper Princess

Silver Falls Series
The Andrews siblings find love in a small town.
The Christmas Window
A Slice of Summer

The Bar V5 Ranch Series
Fall in love at a dude ranch in Montana…
Home for Christmas
Mistletoe Magic
Kiss Me, Cowboy
Mistletoe Wedding
A Christmas Homecoming

Ever After Series
Happily ever after reality TV style…
The Honeymoon Prize
The Cinderella Princess
Christmas in the Castle

Love at the Chocolate Shop Series
Three siblings find love thanks to
Copper Mountain Chocolate…
A Thankful Heart
The Valentine Quest
The Chocolate Touch

Made in the USA
Las Vegas, NV
25 October 2022

58158890R00173